"Joe, we'd better go get showered and changed," I said.

"Right. Don't worry, Aunt Trudy," he added. "We'll have plenty of room for dinner. We're growing boys, remember?"

We went inside before they could ask where we'd been for the last two days. Since the summer began, we'd already been gone several times on missions for ATAC, and I was beginning to run out of excuses.

Joe took a shower, then it was my turn. I was just in the middle of getting dressed again, when I heard a prerecorded tune being blasted on speakers just outside the bedroom window. It sounded like it was coming from an amplified jack-in-the-box, except it was a little out of tune.

I recognized the song right away—"I've Been Working on the Railroad."

Looking out the window, I saw that it was an ice-cream truck. CAPTAIN CREAMY was painted on the side.

I'd seen the truck before. There were always a few of them around town during the summer months— one at the town pool, another at the marina by the bay, and a third near the town hall and library.

The tune played on and on, over and over again. No kids were lined up to buy ice cream—yet the truck didn't move.

Weird . . .

THE HARDY BOYS

UNDERCOVER BROTHERS™

Available from Simon & Schuster

THE HARDY BOYS

BOYS

UNDERCOVER BROTHERS™

#5 Rocky Road

FRANKLIN W. DIXON

Aladdin Paperbacks
New York   London   Toronto   Sydney

ALADDIN PAPERBACKS
An imprint of Simon & Schuster
Children's Publishing Division
1230 Avenue of the Americas
New York, NY 10020

Copyright © 2005 by Simon & Schuster, Inc.

THE HARDY BOYS MYSTERY STORIES and HARDY BOYS
UNDERCOVER BROTHERS are registered trademarks of
Simon & Schuster, Inc.
ALADDIN PAPERBACKS and colophon are trademarks of
Simon & Schuster, Inc.
Designed by Lisa Vega
The text of this book was set in Aldine 401BT.
Manufactured in the United States of America
First Aladdin Paperbacks edition August 2005
10 9 8 7 6

Library of Congress Control Number 2005920484
ISBN-13: 978-1-4169-0006-1
ISBN-10: 1-4169-0006-3

TABLE OF CONTENTS

1.
FISH FOOD

Shark!

He was speeding toward me, his jaws wide open, showing hundreds of razor-sharp teeth. His eyes were dull and dead. They held out no hope for mercy. Clearly, all he saw in me was a great big human Happy Meal.

The shark wasn't the only one who wanted me dead either. Two bad guys in scuba gear, complete with loaded spearguns, were ready to finish the job—if the shark left anything over.

Before I could think about them, though, I had to deal with Jaws.

The shark was closing fast. I ducked at the last second, shoving him away. His sandpaperlike skin brushed hard against my wet suit, shredding part of it—but otherwise, I was still in one piece.

Or was I? No sooner had I dodged him than I realized I couldn't breathe. Looking over my shoulder, I saw that my air hose had been cut. The shark had bitten it clean in half!

I grabbed the free end of the hose, which was gushing bubbles. Removing my mouthpiece, I stuffed the hose directly into my mouth.

Ah. Better.

But only as long as I held the hose in place with one hand. Easy enough, in theory—but now the shark had circled around and was coming back for the rest of me.

This time I'd have to fend him off one-handed.

Luckily, I had my underwater flashlight with me. It's about a foot and a half long and made of superstrong carbonate steel. I pulled it out of the pocket of my wet suit and held it upright in my free hand.

Just as the shark was about to snap his jaws together and cut me in half, I shoved the flashlight into his mouth, as deep as I could. It jammed his jaws open, and he jerked away from me—but not before I grabbed hold of his dorsal fin.

Here we go!

He was pretty furious. I knew if I let go, I'd be swatted into oblivion by his flailing tail.

Holding on was no picnic either. The shark's fin was sharp and rough, and I only had one free hand for grabbing (the other was busy holding the air hose to my mouth). But as long as I didn't let go, I knew I had a chance to survive this nightmare.

I tugged to the right, trying to turn the shark around. And what do you know, it worked! Before I could say "Mayday," Jaws was headed straight for the two guys with spearguns!

They panicked and fired their spearguns at us. Of course, when you're panicking, your aim is pretty miserable. I was counting on them missing— and I was right. The spears whooshed by, doing no harm.

Even better, the two goons had no time to reload. They were too busy swimming for their lives! I let go of Jaws, and he swam after them, still trying to spit out my flashlight.

I had to get to the surface right away, before my air gave out. It wouldn't be long now—my tank had already been near empty when Frank and I were ambushed by those two thugs.

Speaking of Frank—where was he? He'd been right next to me when the fight started.

Uh-oh . . .

Had the shark eaten him before turning its gaze on me?

No! There he was, hiding behind a huge chunk of coral, aiming something at our two would-be assassins. Then I recognized it as the nifty little gizmo we'd brought along on our mission to nab these shark poachers.

Many species of shark are endangered these days, but that doesn't stop the owners of some very fancy gourmet restaurants. They hire poachers, like these two goons, to bring in the forbidden fish.

Frank and I had been sent here to put a stop to it.

Frank fired his weapon, and something shot out in a blur. It exploded right next to the gruesome twosome, opening into a giant net that snared them for good.

Now all we had to do was drag our catch to the surface, where a boat was waiting with a half-dozen police officers on board.

Mission accomplished!

2.

CAPTAIN CREAMY

We motored back to shore on the Marine Police Emergency Team (MPET) boat with our two poachers in cuffs.

It was late August—almost Labor Day weekend. School would be starting soon, and my brother and I would be back at Bayport High, acting like normal kids for a change.

All summer long we'd been involved with one mission after another for ATAC (American Teens Against Crime), the elite teen undercover unit our dad had founded a little while back.

I didn't know about Joe, but I was going to be glad to let things quiet down for a while. We'd had some pretty close calls lately. If you've never come close to dying, believe me—it isn't something you want to repeat often.

Our boat tied up at the dock, and Lieutenant Rogers shook our hands. "Boys, we couldn't have done it without you," he said.

"Don't mention it," said Joe. He meant it too. ATAC is a top secret organization. People find out about it only on a need-to-know basis.

We said good-bye to the crew and walked over to the end of the marina where our rides were parked. Joe and I are the proud owners of a pair of sport bikes you wouldn't believe: lots of chrome, flaming double H's painted on the sides, engines that'll do 14,000 rpm without breaking a sweat, twin front ram-air scoops, and a whole lot of other neat features (some of which wouldn't even be legal if we weren't ATAC agents).

Joe fished out his key and unlocked his seat cabinet. "I don't know about you, Frank, but I've gotta get out of this wet suit and into some dry clothes." He pulled out a T-shirt and a pair of jeans, along with some socks and sneakers.

"Where are you planning to get changed?" I asked.

"How 'bout that gas station across the street?"

I looked over at it. There was a bathroom on the side wall, but it didn't look too clean. Still, if we arrived back in Bayport in our wet suits, our mom and Aunt Trudy would want to know why.

They're not in on the ATAC secret—which makes for some awkward times around our house. Sometimes, we have to out-and-out lie to them, which doesn't feel good at all. But we don't really have any choice—when you're a Hardy, fighting crime comes first.

"Okay," I said, and followed Joe over there. I held my breath while I got changed and washed my hands twice after I was done. Yuck.

Finally, we were back on our bikes and heading home. "That shark nearly got you!" I yelled to Joe over the roar of the wind.

"You're telling me! Lucky I had that flashlight!"

"You know, that's not what flashlights are for."

"Ha, ha! Not funny."

"No? I thought it was a riot! You should have seen the look on your face!"

I was just kidding, of course. I couldn't even *see* his face through the diving mask. Besides, there were all those bubbles from his busted air hose.

I just like yanking my younger brother's chain, that's all. It never gets old.

About an hour later we were back in Bayport. About a mile from home, Joe signaled me to pull over. "I need some ice cream," he announced, parking his bike in front of Mike's Frosty Freeze.

That's Joe for you. Totally impulsive. I have to rein him in sometimes, so he doesn't go totally hog wild.

In this case, though, I didn't try to stop him. Ice cream sounded like a good idea to me. We hadn't eaten since breakfast, and after what we'd just been through, we deserved a treat.

"Rocky Road, double scoop," Joe told the girl behind the counter. Then he turned to me. "Same for you, Frank?"

"You know I can't stand Rocky Road," I said, giving him an elbow to the ribs. "Vanilla, please," I told the girl. "With butterscotch syrup."

"You are such a nerd," Joe told me. "Mr. Plain Vanilla."

"Don't forget the butterscotch," I reminded him.

"Oh, right, the butterscotch—how daring!" He laughed.

I let him have his fun at my expense. I knew I'd get back at him later.

We rode home with our cones in one hand, steering our bikes with the other. Wouldn't you know it, Mom and Aunt Trudy were right out front, weeding the flowerbeds.

"Look at these two, will you?" Aunt Trudy said.

"Don't you kids know better than to ride with one hand?"

"Boys," our mom said, shaking her head. "You know that's not safe."

"Sorry, Mom," Joe said. "We won't do it again, will we, Frank?"

"'Course not," I agreed. "We were just so hungry, and we didn't want to be late getting home."

"Late for what?" Aunt Trudy asked. "Dinner's not till six."

I looked at my watch—it was four o'clock. *Hmmm . . .*

"Speaking of dinner, you boys are going to spoil your appetite, eating all that ice cream so late in the afternoon," Mom added.

"Aarrk! Bad boys! Bad boys!"

Ah, the unmistakable voice of our pet parrot, Playback. I looked up and saw him, perched in the branches of our Japanese maple tree, flapping his wings to show off how beautiful they were.

Playback belongs to all of us. Lately, though, Aunt Trudy has been treating him as her special child (she has no children of her own, even though Joe and I give her plenty to worry about).

"Be quiet," Joe yelled up at Playback. "Nobody asked your opinion."

"Aarrk! Fresh! Go stand in the corner!"

Playback's got a real mouth on him. Joe was about to show him whose mouth was bigger, but I put a hand on his shoulder to stop him. Getting into a swearing competition with a parrot in front of your mother and your aunt is never a good idea.

"Joe, we'd better go get showered and changed," I said.

"Right. Don't worry, Aunt Trudy," he added, "We'll have plenty of room for dinner. We're growing boys, remember?"

We went inside before they could ask where we'd been for the last two days. Since the summer began, we'd already been gone several times on missions for ATAC, and I was beginning to run out of excuses.

Joe took a shower, then it was my turn. I was just in the middle of getting dressed again, when I heard a prerecorded tune being blasted on speakers just outside the bedroom window. It sounded like it was coming from an amplified jack-in-the-box, except it was a little out of tune.

I recognized the song right away—"I've Been Working on the Railroad."

Looking out the window, I saw that it was an ice-cream truck. CAPTAIN CREAMY was painted on the side.

I'd seen the truck before. There were always a

few of them around town during the summer months—one at the town pool, another at the marina by the bay, and a third near the town hall and library.

The tune played on and on, over and over again. No kids were lined up to buy ice cream—yet the truck didn't move.

Weird.

Amazingly, Aunt Trudy hadn't come out of the house to chase the guy away. She was probably back in the kitchen cooking dinner, I figured, and couldn't hear the annoying jingle—at least not as loudly as I did.

Joe came into the room, fully dressed and combing some disgusting green gel into his hair. "That song is driving me crazy!" he said.

"So go down there and tell him to shut it off."

"Me? What about you?"

I rolled my eyes. "Tell you what—we'll both go. That way, if the big bad ice-cream man won't go away, we'll show him our big bad muscles and scare him off."

Spin it like muscle power might be needed, and Joe's there.

We went downstairs and headed toward the front door. Just as we got to it, Aunt Trudy's voice stopped us cold.

"You're not going to eat more of that junk before dinner, are you?"

Mom appeared behind her. "You know, boys," she said in her best librarian voice, "an ordinary ice-cream cone contains eleven teaspoons of processed sugar, along with dozens of other chemicals that aren't the least bit good for your health."

"We weren't actually going to—"

"Kids these days!" Trudy said bitterly before I could finish. "Between the candy, and the ice cream, and the pizza, and the chicken nuggets, and the nachos . . ."

"It's terrible," Mom agreed. "Did you boys know there's an epidemic of obesity in this country? Everybody's gaining too much weight—especially young people."

"We're becoming a whole nation of fatties!" said Aunt Trudy, wide-eyed.

"No more ice cream today," Mom said. "We're having organic vegetables and whole wheat pasta for dinner."

"Yum," Joe said glumly.

It's not that Joe hates healthy food, but Mom has been on this vegetarian thing for the past couple of weeks, and both Joe and I were getting a little tired of green and orange food.

"Okay, Mom," Joe promised. "But we've gotta

get that truck to move before that stupid song drives us crazy."

We went outside and walked over to the truck.

"What can I getcha, fellas?" the guy inside the truck said, leaning out the window.

"Oh, nothing, thanks," Joe said.

"We're not hungry," I added.

"Aw, come on!" the guy insisted. "It's hot out. Gotta cool off with a two-scoop special!"

He looked to be about nineteen years old—tall, with pimples, a long, thin nose, eyes that were a bit too close together, and curly blond hair that stuck out in all directions. His Captain Creamy hat would barely stay on, and he had to keep steadying it with his hand.

"No, seriously," I said. "We don't want any. We just had some ice cream a little while ago."

"Not like *my* ice cream! Try it. Here, have a free sample!"

He grabbed a tiny cone from a stack next to the ice-cream dispenser. "Vanilla, chocolate, or swirl?"

"Nothing. Thanks. Really." Joe was starting to get annoyed. I could see it in his face, but this guy didn't seem to want to take the hint.

"No better way to cool off!"

"Look," I interrupted him. "We don't want any, okay? And we'd like you to move your truck out of here, if you don't mind. That song—it's really annoying."

Captain Creamy seemed offended. "Hey!" he said. "It's 'I've Been Working on the Railroad'!"

"I know that," I said.

"It's a classic," he said. "An American classic."

"I'm sure it is."

"Hey!" Joe broke in. "Just move along, okay? Don't make us have to ask you again!"

"I've got hard ice cream, too!" he kept on. "Toasted Almond? How about a Fudgsicle?"

"Maybe next time," I said.

I felt kind of sorry for him. This poor guy was really desperate.

"Whatsa matter? You don't like ice cream? That's un-American!"

"I guess we're gonna have to call traffic control," I said to Joe, and we turned back toward the house.

"WAIT!"

His shout stopped us in our tracks. "Here!" he said, holding out a big box of ice-cream sandwiches. "Take it—no charge!"

No charge?

"That's weird," I said.

"Maybe," Joe replied, "but the price is right." He went back over to the truck and took the box from Captain Creamy.

"You won't be sorry!"

Joe scowled back at him. "I'm sorry already. Now move along before we call the cops."

This time, Captain Creamy didn't wait around. He hit the gas pedal and, with a screech of rubber, the ice-cream truck barreled off down the street, still blasting "I've Been Working on the Railroad" at full volume.

"We'd better hide this box from Mom and Aunt Trudy," Joe said, looking it over.

"You've got that right!"

"There must be two dozen sandwiches in here. It weighs a ton!"

"We'd better put it way in the back of the freezer."

"I don't think so, Frank."

Joe was looking at me with a suddenly serious expression on his face.

He held up the box for me to see. On the side were written the letters *ATAC*.

Captain Creamy had just brought us our next case!

3.

OVER A BARREL

Well, you could have fooled me.

That geeky ice-cream guy, an agent for ATAC?

No way.

Either they've lowered their standards over at headquarters, or Captain Creamy was the ultimate master of disguise.

Anyway, whatever. We had our next case, and that was what counted.

I went back into the house with Frank right behind me, the big box of "ice-cream sandwiches" under his arm.

Aunt Trudy was waiting, with Playback perched on her shoulder. There was no hiding our prize from them.

"What did I say about junk food?" she asked, shaking her head.

"But Aunt Trudy—," Frank started.

"Aaarrk! Wanna cookie! Wanna cookie!"

"Hand it over," Trudy said.

Yikes!

No way could we let Aunt Trudy look inside that box. I didn't know what was in it, but I knew it wasn't ice-cream sandwiches.

Frank and I were experts at talking our way around our mom, but nobody has ever put anything over on Aunt Trudy.

"We're not gonna open it now," Frank said quickly, holding the box away from her. "We're just gonna put it in the Sub-Zero . . . for another time."

"Hmmph." Aunt Trudy crossed her arms, looking doubtful. "All right. Just as long as you make them last."

Whoa. Impressive. I always knew Frank was a good liar, but you also have to be quick sometimes.

This was *way* quick. Me, I never would have thought of it.

We went down to the basement. Behind us, at the top of the stairs, Aunt Trudy watched, eagle-eyed.

Frank opened the Sub-Zero freezer unit and put

the box inside. "There. Come on, Joe, we've got things to do."

"But—"

"Come *on*, Joe."

I was going to say that whatever was in the box might not take too well to freezing. But Frank was right—what choice did we have with Aunt Trudy there?

We went up to our rooms. They adjoin each other on the second floor, with a shared bathroom in between. Frank and I sat down on the side of my bed.

"Now what do we do?" I asked.

"I guess we wait till Aunt Trudy decides to go to sleep."

"We can't wait till after midnight to check it out—this case could be urgent!"

He shrugged. "Maybe. But we can't risk Aunt Trudy finding out about ATAC."

"Frank, that disk will freeze in there by tonight!"

That got him. "You might be right about that. . . . Just give me a minute to think of something."

He sat there.

I sat next to him.

Nothing happened for what seemed like an hour. Then Frank suddenly sprang up from the bed.

"I've got it!"

"What?"

"It's brilliant. You'll see."

He picked up the phone and punched in a number. "Adam, please."

Adam Franklin is one of the mechanics at our local airport. He's in on the ATAC secret—he has to be, since Joe and I sometimes have to fly planes to weird locations while on our missions.

He also happens to be a friend of Aunt Trudy's.

"Hi, Adam," Frank said into the phone. "Frank Hardy. Listen, I've got a favor to ask of you. What are you doing tonight after dinner? Really? That's great! How'd you like to invite my Aunt Trudy out to the movies? Yes, I'm serious. . . . I know you're not interested in her 'that way,' but couldn't you just pretend for one night? Adam, it's for ATAC. . . . I can't go into it any further, but trust me, it's important. . . . Great! Adam, you're the best. . . . I owe you one. . . . Yes, a *great big* one. Right. You'll call her, then? Excellent. Bye!"

I shook my head in wonder. "You are unbelievable."

"On the contrary. I think I'm totally believable. Ask Adam."

In a few minutes we heard the phone ring downstairs and Aunt Trudy saying, "Hello?"

19

She stayed on the phone for only a minute. But afterward, we could hear her humming a cheerful tune to herself as she got dinner ready.

"Soon as she leaves the house, we rescue our box," Frank said.

"We'd better hope it's not frozen by then."

"It won't be."

"I'm glad you're so sure. Do you know how cold it is inside a Sub-Zero?"

"Let me guess. Below zero."

"Exactly!"

Frank grinned at me. "No worries, bro. I pulled out the plug with my foot and left the door open a crack."

Is my big brother amazing, or what?

After dinner Aunt Trudy raced upstairs—and when the doorbell rang half an hour later, she came back down, all dressed up. Complete with makeup.

(She *never* wears makeup! Adam, you *dog,* you!)

Once she was gone, we quickly retrieved our box. It was chilled, but miraculously, not frozen. I tore the top open and reached inside. My hand came in contact with frozen metal and stuck to it like glue.

"*Ahhh! Get it off me!*" I yelled, pulling my hand out of the box.

Attached to it was the barrel of a gun.

Frank laughed. "That'll teach you not to grab."

He went into the bathroom and came back with our blow-dryer. Plugging it in, he heated up the gun barrel until my hand came free.

"Now let's see what else is in here," he said, shaking the box's contents out onto the bed.

There were more pieces of the gun, although I couldn't immediately figure out how to put them together. It looked like a sawed-off M4 rifle, but there were some extra parts that were unfamiliar.

There was a large wad of cash, too.

"Excellent!" I said, reaching for it—but Frank whisked it away from me in a flash.

"Uh-uh-uh," he said, wagging his finger at me. "This is for our mission."

"So?"

"So, as the older brother, I'll keep an eye on it for us."

I hate it when he pulls rank on me.

"Let's see what it's all about." He grabbed the video game CD that had tumbled out of the box, popped it into our system, and flicked on the monitor.

The startup video began, with menu options strung out at the bottom of the screen.

Over the Edge, the title roared out at us.

In clever animation that seemed totally real, we were at surface level on a roaring river rapids. White water gushed by us so fast, it made me want to duck.

The title letters whooshed by and out of sight. Then the view backed up, and we saw that we were hovering right over a huge waterfall. And not just any waterfall—

Niagara Falls!

The menu options came on the screen, including one that said, "Play Game." I grabbed the control and chose it. The voice of Q.T., our boss at ATAC, began to speak:

"Hello, there, ATAC agents, and welcome to your next mission. What you're looking at is the famous Niagara Falls. It is, as you know, a major tourist attraction. Millions of people visit every year. The Niagara River, which feeds the falls, is also a major source of hydroelectric power for the surrounding area.

"And now, someone is threatening to turn it off, by damming the river at Lake Ontario!

"That would be a major disaster. The waters of four of the five Great Lakes pour through the Niagara River. If they started backing up, it could cause catastrophic flooding throughout the region.

"Only a lunatic would plan and carry out a scheme like this—and only an ATAC agent can stop him. You'll need

to get up there as soon as possible—certainly within twenty-four hours. Time is of the essence.

"We've provided you with cash for your expenses and a stun gun that can be quickly assembled and disassembled. Nonlethal, but effective in temporarily stopping an attacker. This weapon fires projectiles that explode three feet in front of the target, releasing an electrical charge that stuns your quarry until you can subdue him. Instructions for assembly are rolled up inside the barrel. Please destroy them as soon as you've mastered the process. And remember, please use this weapon only if you feel it is absolutely necessary.

"Good luck. You'll need it. This mission, as usual, is top secret. Oh, and also as usual, this program will revert to an ordinary video game CD in five seconds."

The view angle pointed down, straight down the falls, and we started falling with it. Just as we were about to hit the rocks at the bottom, the picture froze and music came on.

Milli Vanilli.

Ugh.

Frank was already at work, reading the instructions for weapon assembly. "This is so cool!" he said.

Frank loves gadgets.

I'm a bit of a spy weapons geek myself.

I could tell we were going to fight over this one.

But not now, because we had to pack our things and get out of town in a hurry.

And of course, we had to get permission from our mother, too.

Easier said than done.

4.

SLOWLY I TURN

Usually, when Joe and I need to go somewhere by ourselves on a mission, our dad helps us "explain things" to Mom and Aunt Trudy. But this time he was out of town, at a retired police officers' convention in New York City.

We were on our own.

I am the brother in charge of making up stories. The thing is, when you start telling lies, there's no end to it . . . and sometimes things go wrong, and you get caught in your lie . . . which means you have to lie some more to get out of it. . . .

You get the picture.

"Um, Mom?" I said as we ate breakfast. "Joe and I want to take one last trip on our bikes before school starts."

"Oh, no," she said. "Not *another* trip!"

Right away I could see she wasn't happy about it.

"I was thinking about what you were saying about junk food yesterday," I said, "and there's this organic food convention starting tomorrow in Niagara Falls."

"Niagara Falls?" Aunt Trudy said, her mouth gaping.

"Aaarrk! Slowly I turn . . . step by step . . . inch by inch . . ."

"Shut up, Playback," Joe warned the parrot.

Playback took the hint, hopping away from Joe and over to the far end of the counter. He could tell Joe meant business. There's a time for joking, and this wasn't it.

"Niagara Falls is nine hours from here!" Aunt Trudy said.

"Now, Trudy," Mom said, "if the boys finally want to do something I approve of, why should I stand in their way? Besides, Niagara Falls is a national landmark—and they've never seen it."

Good old Mom. She's always been cool about allowing us a lot of freedom.

And by the way, just for the record, she was right—with all the cases we've been on, we'd never been to Niagara Falls.

Aunt Trudy wasn't giving up yet, though. "I

don't believe a word of it. And Joe, I don't like you speaking to Playback that way."

"Huh? He's a parrot!"

"Never mind—he's part of our family, and he deserves the same respect we all do. Now, apologize."

Joe looked bug-eyed, like he was choking on a piece of raw liver.

"I think you'd better do it, Joe," Mom said gently.

He looked at me.

I shrugged. "Hey, dude, you were rude to the parrot."

Joe looked at Playback and tried to spit out the words. "I . . . I'm . . . s . . . sorry."

I've never seen him look more miserable. Me, I was cheerful as could be. "So," I asked, "can we leave right away?"

"I'll be sorry to see this summer come to an end," Joe said as we strapped our backpacks onto our bikes.

"It's been pretty amazing," I agreed.

We'd been on at least half a dozen cases, with lots of thrills and chills and narrow escapes.

Now it was almost over. Would ATAC even call us during the school year?

Not very often, I guessed. This might be our last case for a very long time.

We strapped on our helmets and headed for the interstate. The sun was already hot, but it wouldn't matter at 70 mph, with the wind in our faces.

Our plan was to ride straight through till we got there. It was a straight shot up the New York State Thruway.

One thing we didn't plan on was road construction. Between Rochester and Syracuse, traffic was gridlocked. Not that we let that slow us down. We just switched to the service road and rode at 60 mph.

And that's how Joe hit the pothole.

I saw it coming and managed to maneuver around it—but I must have screened it from Joe's view, because he ran right over it. I didn't see him hit, but I heard his cry of pain.

I slowed down as quickly as I could and stole a quick glance back at him. He was still riding, but in standing position.

Ouch. That must have hurt.

Joe was still riding standing up a couple of hours later when we pulled into Niagara Falls. He rode up alongside and signaled me to pull over outside a building marked TOURIST INFORMATION.

"You okay?" I asked.

"I'll never be the same again. Talk about rocky road!"

Well, at least he still had his sense of humor.

We started grabbing maps and brochures off the rack outside the building. "First thing we've gotta do is find a decent hotel, where I can take a long, hot bath," Joe said.

I corrected him. "First thing we've gotta do is check out the falls."

"Aw, man . . . every bone in my body is aching."

"Joe, we got a late start on this as it is. We have to get down there and scope it out, so we know where to start investigating. Otherwise this jerk will have dammed up the river before we can stop him!"

"Here. I pulled this brochure for you," Joe said.

"Over in a Barrel," the title read. It had stories of everyone who'd ever gone over the falls—with or without a barrel.

"What's this for?" I asked.

"I figured this guy must be some kind of nut, right? Well, if you want to know about nuts obsessed with Niagara Falls . . ."

He had a point. I looked through the brochure while Joe went inside and bought some aspirin, which he downed with half a bottle of water.

Quite a few people over the years had gotten the idea of tackling the falls into their heads. Most of them had died.

The most recent jumper, however, a guy

named Kirk Jones, had not used anything at all for protection—and he'd come out alive and uninjured!

It just goes to show you, it's better to be lucky than smart.

I managed to get Joe back on his bike, and we headed straight for the American side of the falls (the other side is in Canada). We parked our bikes, paid our admission fee, and went down an elevator and through a tunnel.

We came out onto a wooden walkway and stared at the most amazing sight I'd ever seen this close up. If you've never been to Niagara Falls, you've got to go—it is totally spectacular!

There we were, not twenty feet away, as mountains of water roared over the edge of the cliff and down past us, where they hit the rocks below and sent clouds of spray back up. At the end of the walkway, stairs led down toward the abyss below.

I fished out the binoculars I always carry and checked out the river below us. There was a boat chugging hard to get as close to the falls as possible. I could make out her name: *Maid of the Mist.*

Cute.

I also saw, across the falls on the Canadian side, a promenade crammed with sightseers. Behind them was a park, and farther down, a main street with all sorts of tacky attractions on it: a wax museum, a museum of famous freaks, a replica of a torture chamber, an instant wedding chapel.

I remembered that Niagara Falls is a famous honeymoon spot. I have to tell you, it didn't seem that romantic.

Maybe it was different after dark.

I lowered my binoculars, and there, on the face of the Canadian cliff, was a hydroelectric energy station. Obviously, Canada was using power from the falls to light up its houses and factories. I guessed that the United States was doing the same.

One more reason why it would be a major disaster if this fiend succeeded in damming up the river!

"Can we find a hotel now?" Joe asked. "I'm about ready to crash."

"Just a few more minutes. I want to talk to the head of security first."

"Aw, man . . ."

I knew Joe wasn't happy, but he followed me down the stairs to the next level of walkways, and then down again until we were almost at the bottom where the falls hit the rocks, became a river again, and flowed toward Lake Ontario.

The *Maid of the Mist* was heading back to Canada now. There were other small boats farther away, but none that could handle being this close to the falls.

How could anyone—with or without a barrel—survive a fall onto these sharp rocks?

I lifted my binoculars to the top of the falls and stared at the rushing torrent as it leaped into the void, then fell. It seemed so close I almost had to stop looking.

That's when I saw something totally out of place.

A *man* was teetering right at the edge of the falls, hopping from boulder to boulder.

Then, as I watched in helpless horror, he jumped!

JOE

5.

INTO THE WHIRLPOOL

I was dog tired. We both were. Try riding eight hours on a motorcycle, hitting the world's biggest pothole, and then taking a walking tour of Niagara Falls.

And just when I'm ready to tell Frank, "Let's call it a day," this guy goes over the edge of the falls!

What he was thinking, I have no clue.

What was *I* thinking? *This cannot be happening. No possible way.*

People started screaming, pointing to the spot where he'd hit. In an instant all my aches and pains were gone. There was only one thing to do, and I didn't have to think about it. I kicked my shoes off, hopped the railing, and jumped in.

I knew Frank would be right behind me. That's

one thing about the two of us. When it comes to saving a life, there's no hesitation, ever.

I was not prepared for the ice-cold water, or for the strength of the current. It swept me away before I knew what was happening. Soon I was swirling slowly toward the Canadian side, then around and back again.

It was a big whirlpool!

I'd seen it from up above, but forgot about it when the time came to jump in. And now all three of us were caught in it.

Great.

Frank and I were strong swimmers, but stronger than a whirlpool? I knew one thing for certain— we didn't have much time to dally.

First things first: Where was the jumper? It was hard to see anything with all the spray and foam, but finally I saw him, ahead of me and to the left. Swimming with the current, which was getting stronger all the time, I caught up to the man's limp body and grabbed hold of it.

I was glad he was out cold, or he might have struggled, making us both go under. This way was easier—I only hoped he was still alive.

Taking his shirt in one hand, I swam with the other, kicking like crazy with my feet. I took an angle that let the current stay behind me, pushing me forward as I slowly tacked to the right—toward the outer edge of the whirlpool.

Where was Frank?

There was nothing I could do for him at the moment. If I let go of the jumper, he'd be a goner for sure. So I just had to hope Frank was okay.

I was willing to bet, though, that Frank could handle himself. I was almost to the edge of the swirling, sucking whirlpool, when the jumper woke up. Right away, he started kicking and screaming, trying to get free of me.

Fat chance. I wasn't going to give him a second opportunity to kill himself—not now that I'd gotten myself soaking wet for him.

Wow, this guy was strong, though. He had the strength of a madman.

Come to think of it, he was one. What had I expected?

Totally panicked, he started grabbing my face, digging in with his fingers.

OW!

Suddenly he stopped and was calm again.

Huh. Weird.

I looked back, and there was Frank, his fist raised for a second blow in case it was needed.

I was totally spent. Frank grabbed my heavy load, and we both made for shore.

The rescue squad was just arriving, together with a cohort of police. There was even a helicopter flying overhead.

Frank laid the unconscious jumper down on the path and sat down to catch his breath. I plopped down alongside him.

"He's still alive," one of the paramedics said. "Let's pump him out before we load him into the medevac."

We watched the professionals do their thing. Soon the jumper was strapped onto a stretcher and ready to go. But the police—not to mention Frank and I—wanted to talk to him first.

Our nut job had finally woken up. He was babbling away, but it sounded like gibberish to me.

"What's your name?" Frank asked him.

He looked up and seemed to notice us for the first time. "Nut," he said.

"I can't believe this!" I said. "*He's* calling *you* a nut?"

"Peter Nutt," the man whispered.

Boy, life is so strange sometimes, you couldn't make it up.

Right away, Mr. Nutt started opening up his heart to Frank, crying his eyes out, saying he wanted to end it all.

I don't know what it is about Frank, but everyone always wants to confess to him.

Anyway, the cops were taking careful notes, and the ambulance guys were getting impatient. But to make a long story short, here's the gist of what our man Nutt told Frank.

SUSPECT PROFILE

Name: Peter Nutt

Hometown: Toronto, Ontario, Canada

Physical description: Age 32, 5'9", 150 lbs., dirty blond hair. Stutters. Usually seen wearing a beret.

Occupation: Being a nut?

Background: Unpublished children's book author who went insane after his masterpiece got rejected the same day Everybody Poops topped the bestseller list. Married. Three children.

Suspicious behavior: You saw it. Is jumping over the falls suspicious enough for you?

Suspected of: Being crazy enough to dam up the Niagara River.

Possible motives: Who knows why nuts do things? And everything about this guy—even his name—is nutty!

I wondered if he was really capable of an organized scheme like damming the Niagara. He seemed like just an ordinary, certifiable nut to me.

But could it really be just a coincidence?

After the ambulance rode away with Peter Nutt inside, still raving, the policeman in charge turned to me and Frank.

"I'm Ned Leeds, Niagara Falls chief of police," he said, shaking our hands. "Thanks for your good work, boys—he wouldn't have made it otherwise."

"Do you think he'll live?" I asked him.

"I'm not a medical man," he said, "but he doesn't look too bad to me."

"Chief Leeds," Frank said, "we're the Hardy brothers, from Bayport. Our dad is Fenton Hardy—you might have heard of him. . . ."

"*Heard* of him? He was the head of the Association of Private Investigators a few years back! Hey, I was at conventions with him—the guy's a legend! And you're his boys, huh? Well, two chips off the old block! What do you know?"

He laughed and slapped us both on the back. I don't know about Frank, but I was sore all over.

"We're actually here about the threat to the falls," Frank said.

"Threat?"

"You know—damming up the river at Lake

Ontario? We were sent here to check it out."

"Well, that's mighty nice of you, boys, but you're a little late."

"What?"

"We locked that maniac up almost a year ago."

"Huh?"

"I'm surprised you didn't read all about it in the papers," he said, laughing and slapping our backs again.

Ouch!

"Oh, yeah, that's right—you're not from around here. I guess it didn't make the front pages as far away as Bayport. But it was big enough around here, I'm telling you. Ha!"

Another painful slap on each of our backs. "So, you fellas came all this way just for that?"

"Yeah," I said, exchanging a disgusted look with Frank. "Yeah, we did."

"You know," Chief Leeds said, suddenly getting serious, "you shouldn't have jumped in after him like that. I mean, it took guts, but you could've been killed. And for what? To save a nut job like that? It would have been a big waste, if you ask me."

Chief Leeds wandered off to talk to his men. We stared after him.

"You think he's telling the truth, Joe?"

"Huh? Why wouldn't he be?"

"I don't know. I'm not sure of anything right now, least of all who to trust."

"Not Captain Creamy, that's for sure. He's the one who gave us the mission."

"Yeah, but Joe, he only delivers what ATAC gives him."

"Well, *somebody* at ATAC screwed up."

"Oh, well. At least we got to see Niagara Falls."

"And saved somebody's life."

"Right."

"Well, great, I feel all warm and fuzzy inside." I made a face and sighed. "Now what do we do?"

"Well, you mentioned a good night's sleep. . . ."

"Yeah. I'm down with that."

Just then, my cell phone rang.

"Yello."

"Joe, it's Dad."

"Oh, hi, Dad."

He didn't sound happy.

"What's up?"

"You and Frank need to get back home right away."

"But Dad, we're—"

"There's trouble in Bayport."

"Trouble? What kind of trouble?"

"I don't want to talk about it over the phone, but

40

it's serious. I'm on my way home. Hurry back. There's no time to lose."

Aw, *man* . . . !

"Can't it wait till morning, Dad?"

"I wish it could, but I think you'd better get right on your bikes."

"Okay," I said. What else *could* I say?

"I'll see you when you get here. Drive safely, son."

Dad hung up, and I turned to Frank.

"You're not gonna believe this, bro. . . ."

6.

HOME AGAIN, HOME AGAIN, JIGGETY-JIG

We didn't hit any more bad potholes on our night-time ride back through the heart of New York State. Still, out of the past twenty-four hours, we'd spent sixteen on our bikes. I was sore all over. Joe, the pothole king, felt even worse.

And then, on top of everything else, it started to rain. About an hour out of Bayport, the skies opened up, and rain started coming down in sheets. Lightning was flashing all over the place.

We had to slow down, along with all the other traffic. During the worst of it, we even took shelter under an overpass. By the time we finally got back into town at six A.M., we were drenched, tired to the bone, and in *very* crabby moods.

In the eastern sky, day was breaking. Although the sun was hidden by the storm clouds, they were blowing away fast, and I could tell it was going to be a beautiful day.

I wished we'd slept in Niagara Falls overnight instead of rushing straight home—but our dad had said the magic words, and we knew there was no time to lose.

We passed a bus stop. The *Bayport Times* truck was just making its morning delivery. It pulled away as we drove up.

"Got any quarters?" Joe asked me.

"Nope. I used them all on the tolls. How 'bout you?"

"Same." He jiggled the door of the dispenser. "Bummer."

I looked over his shoulder at the paper in the dispenser window. LOCAL SCHOOLS VANDALIZED, the headline read.

"Can you believe that?" Joe said. "Our own school system gets hit, and where are we? Hundreds of miles away."

"Bad break," I said.

"Bad break? I'm gonna cream that Captain Creamy guy."

"That kid was just delivering the package, Joe.

Besides, he's an ATAC agent, just like us."

"I guess," he grumbled. "I still want to talk to him about it."

"We'll find him. I'm sure he's around town. Just don't jump all over his case, okay?"

"Me?"

"Joe . . ."

"Okay, okay." I could tell he was still pretty sore about missing the action. He was pretty sore, period.

"Hey, don't sweat it," I told him. "We can still catch whoever did it . . . whatever 'it' is."

"Where do we start?"

"I guess we read the article and find out what happened."

"Okay, let's see. We could jimmy the lock on this thing. . . ."

"Joe, I'm surprised at you."

"Just kidding. Man, I wish we had some spare change!" He banged his fist on the metal box, but the door remained locked.

"I guess we'll have to find out some other way," I said.

"Dad?"

"He may know something. But since this is a school thing, I think we'll have better luck asking Chet. He always seems to know what's going on around school."

"Chet? You *know* he's still asleep."

I smiled. "Yeah, but you *know* how much fun it is to wake him up."

"He . . . hellooo?"

"Yo, Chet."

"Joe?"

"Yeah. Listen, dude, we've gotta meet up."

"Sure. Call me later, okay?"

"Right now, Chet. It's important."

"It's six in the morning. Nothing's that important."

"It's six-thirty, and this is."

With my ear pressed next to Joe's, I could hear Chet yawning through the phone. He's either in training for the Olympic sleeping team, or he should be.

"Wake up, yo!" Joe yelled. I heard Chet screaming as his eardrums were assaulted.

"Okay, okay!" he whined. "Give me a break, will you?"

"Sure, dude. I'll give you an hour. Meet us at the high school. Front entrance. Oh, and see if you can round up Iola and Callie, too. They may know something about this, even if you don't."

"What? Oh, you mean about the school getting trashed?"

"Uh, yeah. That would be it."

"Okay." Another yawn. "See you in an hour."

"Dude," Joe said, "do *not* go back to sleep."

"I won't."

"Do I have to call back to check on you?"

"No, no, I'm up. I'll be there, for sure."

"Cool."

Joe folded his cell phone shut and put it back in his pocket. "Okay," he said, turning to me. "Let's go home and get some aspirin and dry clothes."

Our dad was already out—probably with Chief Collig over at police headquarters. Dad retired a few years ago, but they still call him in for "consultations" every time there's a problem they can't solve.

Mom and Aunt Trudy were still asleep, and we tried not to wake them up. After all the explaining we'd done to get permission for our trip to Niagara Falls, I didn't want to have to explain why we were already back home.

We got showered and changed, and wolfed down some muffins, then headed over to the high school. I had to keep slowing down so Joe could keep up. Every time he went faster than 20 mph, he started to feel it in his sore thighs.

Chet was waiting for us at the locked front gate, along with his sister, Iola, and Callie Shaw—both good friends of ours. The two girls were wearing matching running suits and looked like they'd already done a couple of miles around town.

Chet, on the other hand, was barely awake. His glasses had broken again since we'd last seen him (way back in early August), and they were now held together with a piece of white surgical tape, right between the eyes.

So typical. Chet's sense of fashion is pretty much "seventies nerd." But don't underestimate the mysterious Mr. Morton. He comes in mighty handy sometimes, just when you least expect it.

Right now he had a paper cup of steaming coffee in one hand and half a buttered roll in the other. The other half was in his mouth. *All of it.* I swear.

"Mphmhmgm," he greeted us.

"Nice to see you, too," I said, pulling up and parking my bike.

Joe was right behind me. "Hi, you guys," he said. He gave Chet a little pat on the back of his head. "Hey, pal. Thanks for getting up."

"Did I . . . mphmgm . . . have a . . . mphmgm . . . choice?"

"What is that, a roll?" I asked, breaking off a piece for myself. There was nothing Chet could do to stop me—both his hands were full.

Hey, friends are supposed to share, right?

"Where were you two last night?" Iola asked.

"Niagara Falls, believe it or not," I said. "What did we miss?"

"Someone went on a total rampage," Callie said. "It was like a sicko back-to-school smash-'em-up party."

"They threw rocks through the windows at all three elementary schools," Iola said.

"There's broken glass everywhere," Callie added. "It'll be a miracle if they get it cleaned up and fixed in time for the start of classes."

"What else?" I asked.

"They tore up the grass at the athletic field at the middle school," Callie said, "and here, they stole a bunch of freshly delivered food from the cafeteria."

"All in one night?" Joe asked. "How many of them were there?"

Chet finally finished his roll and joined in the conversation. "It had to have been, like, a coordinated terrorist attack. As soon as the police got to one school, the alarm went off at the next. It was all timed perfectly."

"Hmmm," I said. "Why would anyone attack the school system?"

"Duh, to keep it from opening," Joe said.

"Who would do that?" Chet asked.

"Hello? Any kid who hates school?"

"Wait a minute, Joe," I said. "There may be plenty of kids who aren't thrilled with summer being over, but that doesn't mean they'd go berserk like this."

"I heard it was some janitor they fired years ago who went crazy and escaped from the mental hospital," Iola said.

"Oh, yeah?" I asked. "Who'd you hear that from?"

"Um, Carly O'Brien?"

"Are you kidding me?" Callie said with a laugh. "She is the biggest liar in the whole school. Remember when she said her dad was one of the original Beatles?"

"Well, I was at the Water Cooler at two A.M.," Chet said, referring not to an actual cooler, but an Internet chat room where all the guys in computer club compare notes over the summer. "And *they're* all saying it's the guys on the football team— they're supposedly tearing up the grass so they'll put in artificial turf."

"What a load of garbage!" I said. "People will make up anything!"

"Got any better ideas?" Joe asked me.

I had to admit I didn't.

Man, if only we'd been in Bayport when it happened! Joe and I would have caught whomever it was.

"Well, let's have a look around," I said. "Joe?"

"I'm game."

I fished out my trusty Swiss Army knife and extended the lock pick attachment.

(No, you haven't got one on *your* Swiss Army knife—it's a special edition, given to us by ATAC. Sorry.)

"You sure it's okay to do this?" Chet asked nervously. "I mean, it's technically breaking and entering. What if the principal catches us? Or the police?"

"Relax, Chet," I told him. "We're just fighting crime here. Everyone knows we do that."

True, but they all think we're just amateurs—including Chet, Iola, and Callie.

We went straight to the cafeteria entrance. I could see right away that the lock had been pried off the door—probably with a crowbar. It was now sealed shut with yellow crime scene tape.

"The thief must have brought the food out this way and loaded it onto whatever he or she was driving," I said.

"They would have parked over there," Joe said, pointing to the loading dock.

"Maybe there are footprints," I said, "over there, where the pavement ends."

At the end of the path was a patch of dirt that somebody once forgot to pave over. But the huge downpour early that morning had turned it into a muddy lake. Any footprints that had been there were gone now.

"You think we should go inside?" Joe asked me.

"That might be going too far. After all, the police wouldn't like amateurs like us tramping all over a crime scene."

Joe was smirking. He understood why I'd called us amateurs. I didn't want to blow our cover to our friends. I was telling Joe, in so many words, that the two of us could come back and check things out later—alone.

"Well, it makes it a lot harder to catch whoever did this," Joe said.

"You think it was just a bunch of kids acting like morons?" Callie wondered.

"Kids, probably. Acting like morons, definitely." I crouched down low, staring into space, thinking hard.

"What, Frank?" Joe asked.

"Nothing. It's just . . . there's something so weird about it all."

I stood up again. "I think we ought to talk to Chief Collig, see what the police have found out."

"What about us?" Callie asked.

"Keep your eyes and ears open," I told them. "If anything comes up, let us know right away, okay?"

We went back out to the gate and said our good-byes. Callie and Iola ran off together—they still had two more miles to go.

Chet tossed his empty coffee cup into the garbage can. That's when I noticed that it said "Captain Creamy" on it.

"Hey, did you get that off a Captain Creamy truck?" I asked him.

"Yeah."

"I didn't know they sold rolls," I said.

"Oh, yeah, rolls and coffee, muffins and stuff. Nobody buys ice cream at seven in the morning."

"Where was the truck?" I asked.

"I thought you guys were cutting down on coffee," Chet said.

"Yeah, but we have to talk to the ice-cream man," I said. "He, um, sold us some bad merchandise."

"Really? Well, he was just down the hill there, at the corner of Main and MacArthur."

"Great. Thanks, Chet. See you later." I gunned my bike's engine—it was loud enough to wake the dead.

Chet winced. "Hey, can I get a ride with one of you?"

"Chet," Joe said, shaking his head, "we don't give rides on these. It's not legal."

"Oh. Right."

He waved good-bye as we left him in our dust and headed down the hill to have it out with our friend from ATAC.

JOE

7.

A JOB FOR SUPERMEN?

It didn't take us long to find Captain Creamy. Down on MacArthur, just across from city hall and the court building, there was a line of people waiting for their coffee and reading their morning papers and yawning.

I'd never seen an ice-cream truck this early in the morning—but I could tell it was the one we were looking for, because there was no mistaking that huge head of curly blond hair. With the tiny Captain Creamy hat pinned on top of the pile, the effect was pretty comical.

We waited on line like everybody else. When our friend saw us, his eyes lit up with pleasure. "Back already?" he said cheerfully. "Wow, you guys rule!"

He leaned in and whispered, "Did you solve the case?"

"Um, can we talk?" Frank asked him. "In . . . private?"

Captain Creamy looked out over the line of customers. "Can't it wait? I'm kind of busy here."

"I'm afraid not," Frank said.

"Okay, okay—just give me two minutes."

He rushed through half a dozen orders, then closed his window. The people who were still on line complained loudly, but we really had to have a chat with the Captain.

Frank and I went around to the other side of the truck, up a couple of steps, and through a narrow side door. Inside, it was packed to the roof with a mix of boxes—spoons, napkins, cups—and computer equipment, including tangles of wires that were everywhere.

It was a complete and total mess.

"Man, you should take better care of your business," I said, kicking aside an empty ice-cream box.

"Yeah," Frank agreed, "and that goes for your ATAC business, too."

Captain Creamy looked at us like we were from Mars. "Huh?"

We quickly filled him in on our little trip to scenic Niagara Falls.

"Omigosh! I am *so* sorry—this is totally embarrassing!"

"That's one way to put it," I said. "And just so you know, while we were gone, we missed a crime wave back here in Bayport."

"Really? Oh, man . . ."

Captain Creamy looked like he'd just melted all over himself. "I am such a loser. I don't know what happened. Wait—wait a second . . ." He started pushing around boxes of ice-cream sandwiches until he came to the one he was looking for.

"Look at this, will you?" he said, smacking himself on the forehead. "I gave you guys the wrong case! That box was from the recycling pile—old cases that were supposed to be brought in for shredding!"

Oh, yeah—did I tell you we sent the discs back to ATAC once we'd viewed them? I guess this guy was part of the returns processing arm.

Now I felt bad. He'd messed up big-time, but he hadn't done it on purpose.

"You know," Frank said gently, "maybe if you kept your truck better organized, you could avoid—"

"I know. You're right. I'm a total failure as an

agent." He sank to the floor and buried his head in his hands.

"Hey, man, forget it, okay?" I was sorry now that I'd made such a big stink about it.

"Forget it? That case was a year old! How could I not notice?" He held up the box he'd just fished out. "*This* was the one I was supposed to give you. Here, take it."

"Thanks, " Frank said.

"See, it says 'F&J/H' right there in the corner— your initials. I wrote them in so I wouldn't get it wrong, and I *still* did!"

How did ATAC choose this guy?

He looked like he was about to cry. Still, I needed to ask.

"You're . . . sure this is the right one?"

He nodded miserably. "Sorry," he repeated for about the tenth time. "I've just been under so much pressure lately."

"Pressure?" Frank asked. "What kind of pressure?"

"My mom got laid off last Christmas, and I've had to work odd jobs to help out, instead of going to college so I could have a real career someday. . . ."

"Aw, man, that's rough," I said, patting him on the shoulder. "What about your dad?"

"My dad? Ha. That's a laugh. I haven't seen my

dad since he walked out when I was three." He sniffed. "My mom keeps pressuring me to earn more money and pay my own way. But you know, I'm only twenty."

"What's your name?" Frank asked him.

"Ernie Bickerstaff."

"Ernie Bick . . . hey, didn't you go to Bayport High?"

"Yeah, I graduated a couple of years back."

"I remember you," I said. "You were the guy in the chicken suit at all the football games!"

"Yeah, that was me," he said with a sad smile. "Not a lot of career opportunities for six-foot-tall chickens."

"Doesn't the ice-cream job pay you well enough?" I asked.

"Yeah, but it's seasonal," he explained. "And you know as well as I do that ATAC doesn't pay enough—besides, it's only part-time. I have to do computer consulting on the side just to bring in my share of the rent."

I knew we should report him to ATAC for his mistake—but I didn't have the heart, and Frank didn't either.

"Listen, nobody's perfect," he said.

"Don't worry about it," I added.

"If ATAC hears about this, they'll fire me for sure!"

"Hey," I said. "Nobody's going to tell them, okay? We'll solve this new case, and the one here in Bayport, too—and nobody has to know you messed up."

"Gee, thanks," he said, looking up at us like we were angels from heaven. "You guys are the best—everyone at ATAC says you never fail."

"Everybody fails sometimes," Frank said. "Trust me."

He took the box from Captain Creamy and we left him there, sadder but hopefully wiser.

"We'd better get on this right away," Frank said, holding up the box as we left the truck. "Let's go see what it's all about."

"Starr back to throw . . . he heaves it . . . and it's a touchdown! Touchdown Packers!"

Frank and I stared at the monitor. We're both longtime football fans, so there was no doubt what we were looking at—it was an old film of the first Super Bowl in 1967, between the NFL's Green Bay Packers and the Kansas City Chiefs of the old AFL. The film was grainy and jumpy, and the announcer's voice seemed to come from another era.

Suddenly the film faded out, and in its place was an exterior shot of the Pro Football Hall of Fame in Canton, Ohio.

"*Hello, there, ATAC agents. Welcome to your next case.*"
It was the voice of Q.T.

"*Every year, thousands of fans flock to the Football Hall of Fame to see rare artifacts of seasons past. One of the most popular exhibits features the first Super Bowl trophy, pictured here. . . .*"

The exterior cross-faded into a shot of the golden football, perched on its pedestal. SUPER BOWL I CHAMPIONS: GREEN BAY PACKERS, VINCE LOMBARDI, COACH, was engraved on the base.

Then the screen went black. In a moment we were looking at the trophy again—but it was gone. We saw only the pedestal.

"*Unfortunately, the trophy you are looking at has recently been stolen. News of the theft has been kept secret for the past week—the room is cordoned off as being 'under construction'—but we can't keep up the pretense much longer. You've got to find the trophy and return it to where it belongs! Good luck. And, as usual, this CD will revert to an ordinary music CD in five seconds. Five . . . four . . . three . . . two . . . one . . .*"

Marching band music suddenly blared out of the speakers as the screen went to a still shot of Bart Starr, Hall of Fame quarterback, throwing a long bomb.

"Wow!" I said. "The original Super Bowl trophy! Frank, this is gonna be so off the hook!"

"I don't know," he said. "What about the school break-ins?"

Oh, yeah. I'd forgotten about them. Still, this was a national historic treasure we were talking about! "I'm sure Chief Collig and the Bayport Police can solve the school case without our help."

"If they had any leads, they wouldn't have asked Dad to call us in."

"Well, we could get right on it as soon as we come back from Canton."

"Joe . . ."

"ATAC jobs come first, Frank!"

"I guess you're right," he said. He shook the box, and out came a wad of cash for expenses.

"How much is there?" I asked.

"Not that much."

"Enough for round-trip plane fare?"

"Joe, I'm surprised at you—I thought you liked riding our bikes."

My back and thighs were already aching—and Canton, Ohio, was almost six hundred miles away!

Ouch. This was gonna hurt.

My thighs were already hurting, just thinking about it!

8.
TOURIST TRAP

"You want to go *where*?"

"Canton, Ohio."

After a short nap, we were sitting at lunch with Mom and Aunt Trudy. Dad was in New York for the day again, giving a workshop to three hundred police detectives on youth crime—something he knows more about than most police forces.

"But you just got back from—where was it this time?"

"Niagara Falls, Aunt Trudy," I said.

"We changed our minds about staying there," Joe added.

"Oh, and why is that?" Aunt Trudy asked. She's so nosy sometimes—I think it's because she suspects we're holding back on her. And she's right, really. But she can *never* know about ATAC—it would expose her and the rest of our family to extreme danger.

"Um, the falls were closed for repair," Joe said, before I could stop him. He says the dumbest things sometimes.

"Aaarrk!" Playback squawked from his perch on Aunt Trudy's shoulder. "Slowly I turn! Slowly I turn!"

"So now you're going right back out again? On your motorcycles?" Mom said. "Haven't I shown you the statistics on how dangerous they are?"

Our mom is a superlibrarian. Super, because she knows every fact and figure there ever was—or at least, she can look them up faster than anyone else I know.

"Yes, Mom," I said. "But you know how careful Joe and I always are."

"Bad boys! Aaarrk! Bad boys!"

"Shut up, Playback," Joe said, forgetting his manners.

"Joe! That's terrible!" Mom said, putting her hands on her hips. "I'm shocked—just shocked."

"Apologize right this instant!" Aunt Trudy demanded, swinging her shoulder forward so Joe could tell Playback how sorry he was.

"Sorry," Joe mumbled.

"Now give him a kiss," Trudy demanded.

Playback made kissing noises that sounded horribly real.

"I'm not kissing him," Joe said. "It's not sanitary!"

"Well, just you watch your language in future," Mom said sternly. "And please be careful on the highways."

"Thanks, Mom!" I said. What a relief! As usual, she was letting us have our way.

"I can't believe you're caving in like this, Laura," Trudy said. "If they were my boys, I'd . . ."

But Joe and I didn't hear the rest—we were already halfway up the stairs, on our way to get packed for our next case!

We took off as soon as we could. It was a gorgeous day, perfect for riding. The wind in our faces, the roar of the engines filling our ears, lots of open road . . . I think even Joe enjoyed it, in spite of his aching legs.

But after dark, and dinner at a highway rest stop, we both agreed we couldn't make it all the way to Canton in one shot. "Hotel?" Joe asked hopefully.

I felt the wad of cash in my vest pocket. "Sure, why not?"

"Hotel with hot tub?"

"Now you're pushing it."

"Aw, come on!"

"We're on a budget here, Joe. We might need this money to help track down the Super Bowl trophy."

"You're such a party pooper."

"Take a hot bath instead."

"Not the same thing. Not even close."

He didn't like it, but he knew I was right, so he stopped fighting it. "Okay. First cheap dive we see, we pull in."

Off we went, leaving the highway rest stop behind. Only, we didn't realize there wasn't another exit for thirty-six miles.

The highway wound up into some mountains. It was dark on both sides of the road—no towns, not even any houses. I checked my gas gauge, just out of caution. Good. It was still one-quarter full—it would be a bad thing to get stuck up here, out of gas.

You could be here a long time.

We reached the top of the mountain pass. Here, parked alongside the road, were several trucks pulled over for the night. Their lights were on so you wouldn't plow into them, and they lit up the hillside like it was Christmas.

Joe and I passed a sign that cautioned: STEEP

DESCENT—DANGEROUS CURVES, NEXT 6.3 MILES.

Okay.

We slowed down a little.

That's when we heard the roar of the truck's engine creeping up on us from behind.

I pulled out of the left lane and in behind Joe, so that we were riding single file and the truck would have room to pass us—but why he was going so fast, I couldn't understand.

Hadn't he read the sign?

The incredibly loud blaring of the truck's horn nearly made me lose my balance and have to stop.

I turned and looked over my shoulder. He was less than twenty feet behind us, and gaining fast.

Why didn't he just go around? What was he trying to do, anyway? Kill us?

I quickly started my bike again and sped up, overtaking Joe. "Come on!" I shouted, motioning for him to speed up and follow me.

Then I gave it gas for all it was worth. Joe kept up with me, and we rode side by side just a few feet in front of the monster truck.

Like I said, it was dark out here, and we were going downhill. I remembered the sign had warned of "dangerous curves." Now I saw them, straight ahead.

If we kept up our speed, we were sure to crash

into the trees at the side of the road. If we slowed down, the truck would run us over.

We were totally trapped.

And that's when I remembered a little maneuver Joe and I had practiced in ATAC training.

"Joe!" I yelled. "Parallel park!"

It was the code word for the maneuver—I only hoped Joe remembered it. "On three! Ready?"

He nodded. The curve was right in front of us.

"One, two, three!"

On cue, we swerved into the left lane, then hit our brakes, hard.

The truck zoomed by us as we went into a deliberate skid to slow ourselves even further.

I did a 360 on my bike and came to a stop alongside the guardrail. Then I looked for Joe.

There he was, just behind me. I looked up ahead and saw the truck, skimming the guardrail, sending up a shower of sparks.

And still going.

"Let's go get him!" Joe shouted.

In no time we were back up to speed. Only this time, *we* were the ones doing the chasing.

The truck had a big lead on us. But the driver wasn't speeding anymore, probably because he thought he'd killed us. Joe and I were riding side by side in one lane. He couldn't know it was us—

seeing the two lights, he'd think it was just a car behind him.

We got close enough to where our headlights lit up the back of his truck, and I could read the sign on it: GOURMET SEAFOOD WHOLESALERS.

Suddenly, everything clicked into place. That was the name of the company that had hired the shark poachers—our last case! I got close enough to read the license plate and memorized it quickly. Then I signaled Joe to give up the chase.

"Why?" he yelled.

There was no way I could explain over the roar of the truck and our bikes and the wind. So I just pulled over. Joe had little choice but to do the same. What was he going to do, chase the crazed trucker all by himself?

"Okay, why'd we stop?" he demanded, pulling off his helmet in frustration.

"Think about it, Joe," I said. "He's with the guys who hired those poachers—and those guys mean business. What if he had a gun? All we've got is that taser, and who knows how far it shoots? We'd be no match for him, even if he did decide to stop before we ran out of gas."

"I guess you're right," he said. "But we'd better call in the license plate. I don't like the thought of that guy running loose, looking to cream us."

We got off at the next exit, and soon found Mom's Motel and Truck Stop, where we called the police and reported the incident. After they checked with ATAC to make sure we were for real, the officer on the phone promised to set up a roadblock farther down the highway.

I hung up, satisfied that we could finally relax for the night. But *yeesh.* Close call.

Mom's was billed as "your home away from home," but except for the TV in our room, it was nothing like our home.

"Mom" herself—who worked the counter in the office—had quite a beard and mustache going. She took our money, gave us the evil eye, and handed us our room key.

Oh, well. At least the room was clean and there was enough hot water to fill a tub.

The rest of our evening was quiet and peaceful—especially around midnight, when the officer I'd spoken to called back to say that they'd arrested the trucker, a man with a long criminal history, and that he'd confessed he'd been hired to kill us.

He even told the police who'd hired him.

We slept like the dead that night—but believe me, nobody was happier to be alive than we were.

• • • •

The Pro Football Hall of Fame is defintiely worth a visit. All those incredible fourth-quarter comebacks, the famous goal-line stands, the Hail Mary passes, the trick plays, the blocked kicks, and the hundred-yard runbacks—it's all there, along with plaques for all the players who've made it to football immortality.

Joe and I have never played football for any of our school teams. Dad wouldn't let us. When you're a professional crime fighter, any injuries you sustain have to be the on-the-job kind.

So we run track for Bayport High. I do the mile and half mile, Joe handles the sprints. We're pretty good, and totally focused on our track team. But that doesn't stop us from being *huge* football fans.

Even though it had been a long (and dangerous) trip to Canton, we were excited to see the Hall of Fame and to work on a case involving the NFL and its glorious history.

The only problem was, by this time, Joe's sore legs had stiffened up pretty badly. He was walking like a bow-legged cowboy as we entered the Hall.

Not to sound conceited, but sometimes, when Joe and I go places, we get stares from girls who are checking us out. But now, here were two sets of cute girls checking Joe out—and laughing!

Oh, he saw it, all right, and I know it gave him

great pain. Joe works out like a maniac to build the kind of muscles girls notice—and he hates attracting the wrong kind of attention.

So by the time we walked up to the ticket window, he was in a really, really bad mood. "Two tickets," he said to the cashier, forgetting to say "please."

We consulted our maps and pinpointed the location we wanted: the Super Bowl Gallery. I figured it would be roped off following the theft. That wouldn't be a problem, though. Joe and I always manage to get into places we're not supposed to be.

We passed down a long hallway featuring some unforgettable items—John Elway's jersey, Dan Marino's helmet, Lawrence Taylor's protective cup.

Finally, we came to the gallery we were looking for: "Super Bowl: Game of Champions."

It was open.

Well, surprise, surprise. Everywhere we looked, there were big blow-up photos of Super Bowl heroes and great moments from the games. Videos played highlights over and over again at the touch of a button. And all around the room were the actual trophies from years past.

I looked around for the empty case where the missing trophy from Super Bowl I had been.

I didn't see it. I didn't see any yellow crime scene tape either.

This was getting weirder and weirder. Hmmm . . . maybe they'd been covering up the theft to keep it out of the news?

But why would they do that?

Even weirder, Joe pointed to one of the cases. "Hey, Frank," he said. "Check this out. It says 'Super Bowl I.'"

"It must be a fake," I said. "Let's go check with somebody who knows."

I went up to the guard at the gallery entrance. "Excuse me, ma'am," I said.

"Yes?" She was an older lady with graying hair, and she looked like she'd been here since the building went up. If anybody would know about this, she would.

"We heard something about a theft here?"

"Theft?" She looked alarmed suddenly, like it was news to her. "What's been stolen?"

"Well, according to our information, the trophy from Super Bowl I is missing."

She went wide-eyed and turned to look across the gallery to the display case in question.

"Looks to me like it's still there," she said, folding her arms on her chest and giving me a look like I was the village idiot or something.

"That's the original?" I said.

"The one and only."

"You're sure?" Joe asked.

She frowned at him. "What's the matter? You don't believe me? Why don't you go call up Vince Lombardi and ask him?"

Her sarcasm was pretty obvious. Obviously, we'd been sent out here on another wild goose chase!

Either Captain Creamy was seriously messing with our heads, or someone at ATAC was going totally berserk.

Just then, my cell phone rang. The name "F. Hardy" appeared on the display. I pushed the talk button. "Hi, Dad."

Somewhere in the back of my head, I knew what was coming.

"Where are you two?" He sounded annoyed.

"Canton, Ohio."

"What in the world are you doing there?" he asked. "Didn't I just tell you to come home? That there was big trouble right here in Bayport?"

"I know, Dad, but ATAC sent us out here on an urgent mission!"

"Urgent mission?"

"Except it turned out to be a wild goose chase," I went on. "Just like the trip to Niagara Falls."

"What is going on over at headquarters?" he said, more to himself than to me.

"Beats me."

"Anyway, I called to let you know there's been more trouble here."

"Oh, no."

"I'm afraid so." He took a deep breath. "I . . . can't talk about it over the phone. But you'd better come home right away."

"Uh, Dad . . ."

"You can get here by midnight if you drive straight through. If you're tired, take a quick nap. I'll be waiting."

He hung up, and I looked at Joe.

"I hate to break this to you, bro," I said. "But . . ."

9.

CRIME WAVE

This was getting ridiculous. I don't usually like to complain, but what did ATAC think we were, Ping-Pong balls?

I was raring to go work over Captain Creamy again and force the truth out of him. Either he was the biggest loser ever hired by a professional detective agency, or somebody else above him was.

Or both.

Either way, I sure wanted to talk to him and find out why we were being jerked around. But first things first—I was really worried about what Dad "couldn't talk about," and so was Frank.

Maybe it was just my sore legs, but I spent the whole long ride home talking to myself. Once school started next week, I was going to really get into my classes and take a break from all this stress. This summer had been a backbreaker, with all the cases we'd been on—not to mention these wild goose chases right before Labor Day weekend!

Frank was talking to himself too. I could see his lips moving under his visor as we raced along Interstate 80 toward Bayport.

Dad was home alone when we got back, just after eleven P.M. I wondered for a minute where Mom and Aunt Trudy had gone. Then I remembered—tonight was the big end-of-summer event over at the main library. Mom's the Chief Head Honcho over there, and this was their annual fund-raiser.

Dad was up on the third floor, in his office. No one goes in there without knocking—not even Frank or me—because it's got tons of sensitive ATAC stuff: communications equipment, databases, gadgets, weapons, etc.

You get the idea.

I gave our secret knock. (I can't tell you what it is. Sorry.)

"Come in."

Dad was bent over his desk, trying to assemble—or take apart—what looked like a flashlight.

But of course, it was much more than that.

"This shoots microwaves," he said, holding it up

for me and Frank to admire. Then he pointed it at his cup of coffee and pressed the button. In about five seconds the coffee started to boil.

"Cool!" I said. "Now *that* is a handy-dandy item."

"Can I see it?" Frank asked.

Dad handed it to him, and Frank started fooling around with it. (He's such a science geek.)

"Dude, don't point that thing at me," I said. "I don't want to get nuked."

"Did you invent this yourself, Dad?" Frank asked.

"No, it's a prototype I managed to get my hands on."

"How does it work?" Frank asked.

"I was trying to figure that out myself when you got here. I think the inventor rechanneled the frequencies back on themselves, so the wavelengths reverberate inside the chamber and align themselves before being directed outward."

Frank nodded like he understood completely.

Me, I had no clue what Dad was talking about. In my opinion, the only relevant question is always, "Does it work?" (Phys. ed. and history are my best subjects, in case you were wondering.)

I reached out my hand for the gizmo, and Frank gave it over. I checked it out carefully. It had a really nice feel in the hand, and you could easily fit it in the smallest of your pockets.

"Dad, um, are you gonna be needing this for anything?" I asked. "Because I want to show the kids at school how to heat up the lukewarm excuse for food they serve in the cafeteria."

"Sit down, boys," Dad said. "At the rate we're going, there may not be much of a school to go back to."

"*What?*"

"While you were away, someone went after the school bus fleet."

It took a few seconds for Frank and me to absorb the news. While we sat there stupefied, Dad sketched in some of the details.

"Somebody broke the lock on the gate and got into the bus yard. They smashed several windshields, slashed tires, broke headlights, taillights. . . ." He sighed heavily. "It's a disaster. But I think Chief Collig can paint a better picture for you. I've asked him to meet us there in fifteen minutes."

"When did you do that?" I asked, surprised.

"I saw your headlights coming up the street."

Good old Dad—he always likes to show us that, even though he's old, he's still one step ahead of us.

He got up and grabbed his sport jacket off the back of the chair. "Come on. I'll take you down to the bus yard and let Chief Collig walk you over the crime scene."

We followed him downstairs and into his Crown Vic, and we drove off in the direction of downtown.

"Dad," I said, "I know we're in the middle of something else right now, but when you get a chance, could you check with somebody at ATAC about the bad cases we've been getting sent out on?"

"Huh?"

Frank and I filled him in on Niagara Falls and Canton, Ohio—he'd been gone in between, so we hadn't gotten the chance till now.

"I'll have this kid in the ice-cream truck checked out," he promised, "but I know we do have an agent working an ice-cream route in Bayport."

I frowned. It had to be our friend Captain Creamy. No way would ATAC hire two agents to work ice-cream routes in the same town.

"Oh, by the way, boys—one more thing before we get where we're going. I don't care what instructions you get from ATAC. From here on in, until this Bayport crime wave is cleared up, I don't want you leaving town for anything. Understood? Not even to stop a nuclear war."

We didn't need to be told. After missing two straight Bayport crime sprees, we weren't about to go *anywhere*.

．．．．

The bus yard was mostly in darkness. The gate was sealed off with yellow crime scene tape. The whole place seemed eerily deserted.

Then we saw the police cruiser approaching, its flashers going full tilt.

Chief Collig got out of the passenger side and stood up, stretching. Our old friend Officer Conrad Reilly emerged from the driver's side.

"Hello, Ezra," Dad greeted the chief. "Hello, Con."

"Fenton. Boys." The chief shook hands all around, and so did Con Reilly. We'd all worked together before, plenty of times. Nobody knew better than these two how involved the Hardy guys were in fighting crime. They even knew about ATAC.

"Come on in," the chief said, ripping the crime tape and pushing open the gate. "Con, give us some light."

Reilly went back inside the police car and turned on the high beams. Suddenly, the bus yard was lit up like a Christmas tree, except that it wasn't lights sparkling everywhere—it was a million tiny shards of glass.

The ruins of the school bus fleet floated on a sea of broken glass. Yesterday, these dozens of buses had been ready to roll—cleaned, inspected, and cleared to haul Bayport's kids back to school for another year of classes.

Today there was only wreckage.

"How are they gonna start school on time?" I wondered out loud.

"No way, José," Frank said. "It's not happening."

"Sure wish you'd all been around when this went down," the chief said.

"Too late for regrets," Dad said. "I'm putting the boys on this one, all right, Ezra?"

"Good with me," the chief said. "I can use all the help I can get."

"Can you fill them in on what happened? I've got to—"

Just then, there was a sudden movement from the far side of the yard. A figure darted out from behind one of the buses and ran into the shadow of another.

"Somebody's here," Con Reilly said, cracking his knuckles. "Let's go get him!"

10.

A POOR WAYFARIN' STRANGER

It's amazing how fast a person can forget that his legs are in pain. You should have seen Joe take off after the intruder.

I was right on his heels. It took us about thirty seconds to reach the far end of the yard. When we got there, our quarry was nowhere in sight.

I turned around and saw that the adults were only about halfway to us. If Joe and I didn't catch the trespasser, no way were _they_ going to.

"He's in one of these buses, probably," Reilly said.

"We'd better search 'em, one by one," said Chief Collig. "Joe, you and Frank start on the front end. We'll go from here."

I know he just wanted us to travel the farthest.

He, Reilly, and even my dad were still breathing pretty hard.

Joe and I headed back, past rows of parked buses. We split up, working each row from the ends toward the center.

As it turned out, it was me who got lucky—if you want to call it that.

I stepped onto a bus and was halfway to the rear when a wild-eyed, scruffy-looking guy jumped out from behind a row of seats and lunged at me! I dodged him, falling back onto a pair of seats. Before I could recover, he was past me and headed out the front door.

"Joe!" I shouted, hoping he could hear me. "Over here!"

I ran out of the bus after the intruder and caught a quick glimpse of him darting behind another bus. When I got there, though, he'd vanished.

Where could he have gone to so quickly, I wondered?

Suddenly, I heard something moving near my feet. I lay down—carefully, to avoid being cut by broken glass—and looked underneath the bus.

There he was!

"Joe!" I cried as the guy backed away from my grasp.

He was just about to get away again when Joe showed up on the other side of the bus, blocking his way.

"Nice going!" I said.

We had him trapped between us under the bus. He wasn't going anywhere, and he knew it.

"Wait!" he whispered, his eyes darting every which way. "Don't beat me up—I'll give you anything you want—I've got money . . . not *on* me, but buried near here. You can have it—all of it—just let me be."

"Hey!" I said. "Calm down, will you?"

"You're gonna set me on fire, aren't you."

It was a statement, not a question. He was sure we were going to do it. I could see the naked fear in his bloodshot eyes.

"What are you talking about?" Joe said. "Set you on fire? Are you crazy?"

"Ha! That's what they told me at the shelter! Said I was crazy and couldn't stay there—had to go to the hospital for treatment. I ain't getting no treatments—they'll put a computer chip in my head or something."

"We're not going to hurt you," I told him.

"You're here with the cops, aren't you? I saw you with them."

"We're not cops," I assured him, but he didn't seem convinced.

"Who *are* you, anyway?" Joe asked.

"Name's Guthrie. George Guthrie."

"What are you doing here?" I asked. "Did you do all this to the buses?"

"No!" he said in a hoarse whisper. "I didn't do none of it! I was just sleeping . . . sleeping in one of the buses . . . I've been doing that all summer. Found a place where the fence is bent back, and a bus with a broken window lock, and I had it good the last two months. And where's the harm in it, I ask you? It's a lot safer than sleeping out on the streets!"

I guessed he was right about that. But it was still breaking the law, and I told him so.

"I know, I know," he moaned, "but can't you give me a break? I sure could use one, fellas. Think about it—the only breaks I've ever had in my life have been bad ones. And the cops will lock me up for sure! They'll think I did it!"

George Guthrie and Peter Nutt—that made it *two* weirdos Joe and I had chased down in less than a week.

As I lay there under the bus, taking in the rank smell wafting off Guthrie's clothes, I wondered if there was some weird new virus going around, turning normal people into raving maniacs.

"Listen, George," I said, using his first name to

SUSPECT PROFILE

Name: George Guthrie

Hometown: Bayport

Physical description: Age—somewhere in his forties or fifties (hard to tell), 5'7", 150 lbs., long, greasy, uncombed hair (can't tell what color). Wild eyes that keep shifting everywhere in terror. Clothes stink to high heaven—you sure wouldn't want to be wearing them.

Occupation: None

Background: Grew up in foster homes, spent time in reform school for stealing a banana—claimed he was hungry. Never married.

Suspicious behavior: Trespassing, fleeing from the police. His presence at the crime scene doesn't look good for him.

Suspected of: Wave of vandalism against Bayport school system

Possible motives: A mystery—maybe to get even with kids who got better breaks in life than he did.

try and calm him down, "you've got to trust us. We won't hurt you, and neither will the police. They just want to know who did all this damage."

"It wasn't me! I swear it!"

"I believe you, George," I said. The truth was, I didn't know what to believe, but I wanted him to feel safe. "So does my brother here. Don't you, Joe?"

"Huh?"

"*Don't you,* Joe?" I said again. (He's a little thick sometimes.)

"Oh. Yeah. I believe you, too, George."

"Why don't we just get out from under here," I suggested, "and you can show us where you've been living. We won't turn you over to the police until you've had a chance to tell your side of the story, okay?"

"I . . . I guess so," he said.

He led us silently to an undamaged bus, with a concrete block positioned under an open window. We climbed inside one by one. Looking back out the windows, I could see our dad and the two police officers searching other buses and taking notes.

Inside our bus, George Guthrie's summer home was laid out before us. Old, filthy clothes, a large ratty blanket, empty soda bottles.

You get the idea. *Yuckyville.*

It smelled awful, but other than that, this bus hadn't been damaged. If Guthrie had wrecked all those other buses, he'd certainly spared his own.

"George," I said, taking a seat (they didn't look too skeevy) while Joe stood at the front door, "we don't have much time. You've got to come clean."

"You sure you're not with *them*?" he asked, meaning the police.

How was I supposed to answer *that* one?

Easy. I didn't.

"George, tell us the truth—did you damage all these buses?"

"I already told you, it wasn't me!"

"Then you've got to tell us who it was!"

"How should I know? I was dead asleep the whole time!" He grabbed my shirt in his two hands and shook me. "You've got to believe me!" he shouted.

That shout must have gotten the others' attention, because suddenly Joe said, "Here they come."

"NOW, George!" I yelled right in his face. "Tell us what you saw!"

"I didn't see nothing, I tell you! I was drunk! Dead drunk—I only woke up when I heard the glass shattering!"

"And then what happened?"

"Well, I tried to see what was going on, but by the time I got up, they were on the other side of the lot. I was just glad they didn't hurt me."

"*They?* You think it was more than one person?"

"How should I know? I couldn't see a thing, it was so dark—and besides, I need glasses bad. My eyes ain't what they used to be."

"Did you hear anything unusual—besides the breaking glass?" I asked.

"I don't hear so good, neither," he said sadly. "And the cigarettes is killing my lungs—I tried to quit, but with all them butts lying around, it's too tempting."

He coughed to show us how bad his lungs were. His breath nearly knocked me over.

"Okay, George," I said. "I believe you."

And I did. This guy seemed more pathetic than dangerous.

The police forced open the door of the bus and climbed on board, followed by our dad.

"Good work, boys!" Chief Collig said, fishing out a pair of handcuffs.

Bad move.

"You *are* with the cops!" George screamed, jumping to his feet and pointing at me in fury. "I knew it! You kids set me up! I've been framed! Framed, I tell you! Help! HELP!"

"Take him downtown to headquarters, Con," the chief said.

"Wait!" I held out a hand. "Hold on a second,

Chief. This man didn't vandalize any buses. Joe and I will vouch for him—won't we, Joe?"

Joe gave me a look that said, "Are you insane?" But he went ahead and agreed. "Yeah, he's harmless."

"You boys talked to him?" Chief Collig asked.

"Uh-huh," I said. "He doesn't know anything. He was drunk and passed out."

The Chief looked at Dad. "Fenton?"

"Well, if the boys feel that strongly about it, I'd go with their instincts, Ezra."

Good old Dad—I've got to hand it to him, he always sticks up for us.

"Well, it's against my better judgment," the chief said. "But if he turns out to be our man, I guess we can still book him later—for trespassing, if nothing else."

"He needs help more than he needs prison," I said.

"Yeah, how about the town shelter?" Joe asked.

"NO!" George shrieked, trying to leap out the window and escape. "No shelters!"

"Hey, fella," Con Reilly said. "Where do you think you're going?" He grabbed hold of George like he was a stuffed doll, dragged him back into the bus, and snapped a pair of cuffs on him. "If the chief says you're going to the shelter, you're going to the shelter."

"You'll be sorry!" George shouted. "You'll all be sorry! I'm done for! They'll poison me there! I'd rather go to jail, I tell you!"

They had to drag him out of the bus and into the backseat of the cruiser.

When they were gone, the yard was quiet. Dad turned to us and said, "Well, it's been a long day. You boys must be tired."

Tired? Try exhausted. Settling into the plush seats of our dad's Crown Vic, I was fast asleep long before we got home. I'm pretty sure Joe was too.

Tomorrow would be another day. Tomorrow we would start hunting whoever had declared war on Bayport's schools.

No matter what wacko cases ATAC and Captain Creamy gave us, we were *not* leaving town again till this case was solved.

"You really think George was innocent?" Joe asked me over breakfast.

It was already ten in the morning. Mom, Dad, and Aunt Trudy had let us sleep late. Mom was already off at the library, and Aunt Trudy was out in the backyard, gardening. Playback sat on her shoulder, squawking loudly every time she pulled a weed.

"Yeah," I said. "Don't you think so?"

"I don't know what to think, Frank. I mean, the guy's totally gonzo, so who's to say?"

"True. But even the most gonzo of gonzos has a reason for what they're doing. It may be a crazy reason, but it's still a reason."

"Okay, how's this, then?" Joe said. "Suppose George figured that if he managed to put off the start of school, he could live in his bus a while longer."

"That *is* crazy."

"So is George."

"Fair enough. But what you said is really intriguing."

"Intriguing? Wow. You don't usually compliment my ideas that much."

"Don't I?"

"Not too often."

I smiled at him. "Oh, well. I like this one."

"Which one?"

"The one you just had. Forgot it already?"

"How do I know unless you tell me which one it is?"

"You said George might want to prevent the start of school. But you could also say that about other people. As a motive, it ties together both Bayport crime sprees. Pretty neatly too."

"Thank you, thank you."

92

"Notice something else, Joe—the crimes have only taken place during the summer, when schools are empty and buses are idle."

"So?"

"So whoever it is, they don't seem to want to hurt anybody."

"Well, that's good."

"Yeah, but they're still willing to do an incredible amount of damage to property just to keep the schools closed."

"You have to admit, George does fit the profile," Joe said, going back to eating his cereal.

"Yeah, but I'm sure we can come up with other suspects who have the same motive."

"Like who?"

"I don't know. Let's think on it for a while."

Just as I was lifting a spoonful of cereal to my mouth, Joe jumped up and pounded the table—so hard he made me spill the cereal all over myself.

"Hey!" I complained.

"Frank, I've got it! Who do we know who hates school worse than poison?"

I dropped the spoon and rose to my feet, as the light bulb went on inside my brain.

"Of course!" I said. "*Brian Conrad!*"

11.

THE BAD SEED

Let me tell you a little something about Brian Conrad, okay?

He is just possibly the worst human being in Bayport.

Certainly and without question, he is the single worst human being in the entire history of Bayport High.

And just to highlight his sheer awfulness, he has the most gorgeous, sweet, good-natured—oh, and did I say cute?—sister you could ever imagine. That would be Belinda Conrad.

But more about her in a minute. . . .

First, a little more about our newest—and likeliest—suspect.

It was a beautiful morning. Frank and I were

SUSPECT PROFILE

<u>Name:</u> Brian Conrad aka Slimebag, Dirtball, Scuzzbucket, etc.

<u>Hometown:</u> Bayport

<u>Physical description:</u> Age 17, 6'2", 210 lbs., short blond hair. Dresses like a jock, because that's what he is.

<u>Occupation:</u> Being the worst human being in Bayport.

<u>Background:</u> Grew up in Bayport. Somehow became a total jerk, and still is one. Hobbies rumored to include pumping iron; setting minor fires; and torturing small animals, high school freshmen, and anyone smaller or weaker than he is.

<u>Suspicious behavior:</u> A history of vandalism, including triggering false alarms at school, slashing book bags, and breaking into lockers. He's been suspended more times than anybody can count.

<u>Possible motives:</u> Who knows what makes a punk like Brian do the things he does? But he sure hates school with a passion (it's amazing they haven't expelled him yet), and he might go to great lengths to delay the new school year. Also, he might like the idea of getting even with school authorities.

<u>Suspected of:</u> Wave of vandalism against Bayport School system.

having breakfast. Just a normal late-summer day with a normal family (well, almost). Dad was nowhere to be seen.

For a few minutes I totally forgot about crime fighting.

But only for a few minutes. When you're a Hardy, and there's an unsolved case, there's no way you can think about anything else for long.

As soon as we were done washing the dishes, Frank and I took a pitcher of OJ, a couple of glasses, and a pad and paper out to the backyard. We sat down at the round glass table, shaded by its umbrella, and started to sort things out.

"Joe, do you think it's possible Brian Conrad was the one who sent us out of town on those wild goose chases?"

"Huh? No way," I said. "How could he do that? He's not in ATAC."

We both froze for a second.

"No."

"Get out."

"There's no way he's an ATAC agent."

Okay, so we agreed on that one.

"What about that Captain Creamy guy?" I asked. "Isn't Dad supposed to be checking him out?"

"Dude, it's only the next morning. Dad's not Superman. Give him at least a few hours."

"Okay. And what about George Guthrie?"

"What about him?"

"Well," I said, "if the police were going to make an arrest right now, it would be him. That's the way the evidence points."

"Right. But then there's Brian. I don't think we can afford to ignore him."

"This morning would be a good time to catch him at home," I said. "He's a late sleeper, right?"

"True—he's always missing first period."

"So when there's no school, he probably sleeps till at least ten."

"Oh, till noon, man."

"Right. Probably. So we should go over there, right?"

"Um, well . . ." Frank hesitated, and I knew right then what he was going to say next.

"I think you'd better go over there and handle it yourself," he said. "You know how much Brian hates my guts."

It was true. Brian Conrad hates basically everyone, but he reserves a special place in his sick, shriveled heart for Frank.

Why Frank? Could be because Brian's sister, Belinda, *likes* Frank so much.

Yes, that's right—the superfine Belinda has a monster crush on my brother. Has for years.

It kills me, to be honest with you. I can't understand what it is about Frank. It's *insane!* Girls pay a lot of attention to me, normally. But the minute he walks into the room, it's like I don't exist anymore.

Lucky for me Frank has no clue how to handle it. He turns into a raging geek so fast, it's hilarious.

Especially around Belinda. Which was why he was now asking me to go over there and tackle Brian Conrad all by myself.

"Okay, dude," I said with a laugh and a shake of the head. "If you're chicken, you're chicken."

"It's not that I'm chicken."

"Of course not."

"It's just that if I went over there, it could get ugly. There's bound to be a scene."

"Okay. If you say so."

"It has nothing to do with Belinda."

"I'm sure."

"Shut up!"

"Buck-buckaw!" I said, flapping my elbows chicken-style.

Frank punched me in the arm. Just in fun, mind you, but it still hurt. For someone who doesn't spend much time lifting weights, that dude is *strong*.

After looking up the address in the Bayport High Student Directory, I left Frank behind and headed over to Casa Conrad on my bike. I was still sore from all the riding we'd been doing, but it was a fairly short trip—just the other side of the tracks, in fact.

The Conrad family lives, it turns out, in a not-too-shabby part of town. Most of the houses on their street are well cared for, even if they are kind of small.

But not the Conrad house. I spotted it from way down the block, and knew it had to be the place.

The junked car in the front yard was my first clue. The laundry flapping on the clothesline, the peeling paint, the taped-over windows, the garbage strewn all over the lawn, were all proof that Brian lived here.

"The bad seed," as I like to call him.

I took a deep breath of fresh air—the last I was likely to inhale for some time—and knocked on the front door (there was just a hole where the doorbell used to be).

The door swung open, and there stood a fire-breathing dragon. No, not really. It was only Brian and Belinda's mom—but she had a smelly cigar in her hand, and her eyes and face were red and swollen. She'd either been drinking or crying, or else she was just plain poisoned by the cigar smoke.

Whatever.

She took in the sight of me as if I were a six-foot-tall cockroach and said, "Yeah? Whaddaya want?"

"Um, I was looking for Brian?" I said, trying not to use too much breath. Otherwise, I might have to inhale.

"Oh, yeah? And who are you?"

Only now did I notice that she had a toilet plunger in her free hand—the one that wasn't holding the cigar. I knew instantly what it was for: bopping unwelcome visitors (like me) over the head.

"I'm Joe Hardy—a classmate of Brian's."

Obviously, no classmate of Brian's had ever come to his house before, and I could see why not. The place looked like a bomb hit it, his mother was a repulsive witch . . . and that was just the beginning.

Mrs. Conrad moved aside to let me in. Just as I stepped past her into the hallway, she yelled right in my ear: "HEY, BRIAN! SOMEONE'S HERE TO SEE YOU!"

I saw Brian's head poking out of a doorway at the top of the stairs. "Shut up!" he yelled at his mother before spotting me.

My presence seemed to throw him off balance, but only for a second. "Well, well, well," he said as an evil grin spread over his mean, ugly face. "Joe Hardy. What do *you* want?"

"Just to talk. I have a few questions I want to ask you."

"Me? You sure you aren't here looking for my sister?"

"No," I assured him. "But tell her I said hi."

He snorted. "Yeah, right. I'll be sure to do that."

"Hey," Brian's mother said to him, "I wasn't expecting visitors. You wanna have visitors, you better clean up this dump."

Brian sneered at her, then back at me. "Come on up, Hardy," he said. "We can talk in my room."

"It's your mess—you clean it!" his mom screamed at him as I went up the stairs.

Ugh. If I say pigsty, you won't get how truly disgusting Brian's room was. I didn't dare sit down, either on the chairs or the bed. Old food was everywhere, with flies dive-bombing it . . . you get the picture.

Dead things were pinned to all the walls. Insects, sure, but also mice, small birds, and some larger things that were hard to identify, but might have been squirrels.

Oh, boy. This kid was truly *demented*.

"So where's your brother? Where's Mr. Lover Boy?" he asked, shutting the door behind us.

"He couldn't make it."

Brian laughed. "Oh, yeah, sure—he's just afraid

I'll ram his nose into his skull, that's all." Then he looked me up and down. "So he sends you to fight his battles for him, huh? I guess you've got more guts than he does."

"I'm not afraid of you, if that's what you mean."

"Well, maybe you should be."

He cracked his knuckles menacingly.

"I didn't come here to fight you, Conrad," I said. "I came to ask you a few questions about stuff that's been going down."

That caught him by surprise. "What stuff is that?"

"I thought you'd know all about it."

"I haven't got a clue. Why don't you tell me?"

I folded my arms on my chest and waited.

"Okay, okay," he said. "I did hear something about school buses and some other stuff. Is that it?"

"You heard about it?"

"That's right."

"From who?"

"Like I would ever tell you." He laughed and shook his head. "Listen, Hardy, if you think I did something naughty, why don't you tell your friends the cops, so they can come arrest me?"

No, Brian doesn't know about ATAC—of course he doesn't. But everyone at Bayport High knows Frank and I are amateur detectives. Our relationship with the local police is an open secret.

"It's because you've got no evidence against me. Nothing. Nada. Zilch. Am I right?"

He had me, and he knew it.

Luckily, just at that moment, the door to his room popped open and Belinda poked her gorgeous blond head in. "Joe! Hi! I thought I heard your voice!"

"Hi, Belinda," I said, a dreamy smile coming over my face.

She is *so* hot. Not even the presence of Brian could ruin that moment for me.

"Where's Frank? Did he come with you?" she asked hopefully, looking around the room for him.

"Um, not this time," I said, and watched the light go out of her eyes.

"Oh. Well, tell him I said hi, okay?"

"Sure."

"Bye. I've got to go to my voice lesson."

Yeah, she sings, too. Like a bird. Amazing, isn't it, how such an awful house can contain someone like Belinda? It's like they stole her from some other family and brought her home to brighten their dismal lives.

Actually, that's not so far-fetched. Not once you've been to their house.

Belinda's brief visit seemed to put Brian in a bad mood. As soon as she was gone, his phony smile vanished.

"You know, Hardy, you've got some nerve coming over to my house like this." He started advancing on me. His hands were balled into fists, and I expected to see them fly at me any second. "I want you to know, I don't like being accused of stuff." He pounded his fist down on an end table, sending stuff crashing to the floor. "I'm *always* being accused of stuff! *Always!* Even when I didn't do anything. It's totally unfair!"

I didn't back down. "It just seems to me and Frank that whoever is trashing school property doesn't want school to open on time. And we figured you fit the bill."

He grabbed me by my shirt and slammed me into the door. "It's you and your brother's fault I'm always getting blamed for everything! Because of you, I've got a bad reputation at school!"

"Oh, I see. You had nothing to do with it."

I knew I was risking a punch in the face, but I just had to say it.

"Shut up!" he screamed.

I did. He was mad enough already.

"Sure, I hate school," he said, his face inches from mine. "But you know what? Staying at home is even worse! It's dead boring, and it's depressing the heck out of me! I can't wait to go back and start annoying the teachers and kids again."

Guess what? I believed him.

Being in the Conrad house *was* the most depressing ten minutes I'd spent in years. I couldn't imagine how Belinda put up with it. No wonder she joined every club at school and was always taking lessons outside the house!

The poor kid . . .

"Now you get out of here," Brian whispered in my ear, "before I—"

"HEY, BRIAN!!"

His mother's voice shook the whole house.

"WHAT?!"

"GET DOWN HERE AND HELP ME PLUNGE THE TOILET!"

Oh. So *that's* why she was holding the plunger!

"DO IT YOURSELF!"

"I SAID GET DOWN HERE! NOW!!!"

Brian's frustration boiled over. As he left the room, he gave me a shove and released my shirt. I slammed into the doorway, but at least I was free now.

Free to go.

Free to get out of there and breathe again.

"Thanks for your time," I told him as I followed him down the stairs.

"Yeah, and don't come back!" he said. "You're lucky I let you off so easy. Next time you won't be so lucky. Now run along home before I change my mind and make you pay."

I took my time getting to the front door. Nobody was going to make me hurry.

I was going to show him I wasn't scared of him. I let myself out the door to the sound of a toilet flushing.

Out on the front lawn I took a deep breath of fresh air. You know, you never really appreciate air until you're forced to breathe something else—like whatever was perfuming the inside of the Conrad house.

I turned and walked toward the curb, where my bike was still parked.

"Hey, Hardy!"

It was Brian's voice, calling to me from behind. I turned and saw him positioned at the front door—with a gun in his hands!

This is it! I thought. *I'm going to die. Right now.*

I was hit before I heard the shot. Smack in the center of my chest. The impact sent me rocking backward, and I tumbled to the ground!

I looked down at my shirt. It was splattered and soaked in red.

But why wasn't I dead? Why didn't it even hurt?

And then I realized—it was a *paintball* gun!

I shook my fist at Brian, who was cackling with glee, laughing his fool head off.

I felt like strangling him. But I could hear my father's voice in my ear, telling me to be smart. And my mother's, telling me not to let my feelings get the better of me.

Yeah, I felt like killing him. And I could have too.

But instead, I got on my bike and rode away, with Brian's laughter echoing in my ears.

12.

DEEP FREEZE

When Joe walked in the door, I thought he'd been shot. All that red paint sure looked like blood—at least until you looked at it closely.

But Joe wasn't hurt, he was just angry. And when he told me what Brian had done, I was even angrier.

"We could have him hauled in by the police for that. Let's do it, Joe. Let's call Con Reilly and have him put the cuffs on Brian, take him down to headquarters, and grill him for an hour or so."

For once, it was Joe calming me down, instead of the other way around. "Come on, Frank, what good would that do? You think it's going to teach Brian not to be such a dillweed?"

"It would serve him right, anyway."

"Sure, but he'd only come back worse than before."

"True. I guess you're right. What would be the use?"

"There you go." Joe took off his paint-soaked shirt and threw it in a plastic bag for neat disposal.

"You know, Joe, if he's the one behind all the vandalism, it would mean reform school for him."

"You think Brian can be reformed?"

"Mmmm . . . maybe not. Anyway, now that you've talked to him, do you think he did it?"

"He sure got insulted when I suggested it," Joe said, taking a washcloth to himself.

"Truth hurts."

"He actually said he couldn't wait to go back to school."

"And you believe that?"

To my total surprise, Joe said, "Yeah, I think I do. Spending the whole summer at his house would be pretty depressing."

I had never been to the Conrad house. But I found it hard to believe Brian would rather go to school than be there.

"You know," Joe said, pulling a fresh T-shirt over his head, "we should go back to Bayport High and have another look around. We never did go inside the other day."

"The whole place is probably all cleaned up by now," I pointed out. "We should have gone in before the trail went cold. We had our chance."

"Yeah, but all our friends were there. It would have been very uncool to break in with them there."

"We trespassed on school grounds and didn't think anything of it."

"Yeah, but there's breaking the law, and then there's *breaking the law*."

"Why, Joe. I'm surprised at you," I said with a laugh.

"Come on, you dweeb," he said, giving me a little shove. "Let's get over there. Maybe there are still some clues left to find."

The yellow crime scene tape was gone from the cafeteria entrance. A new lock had been installed, and a new coat of paint slapped on to cover the scratches the crowbar had made. "Whoever broke in here," I said, "sure didn't know how to pick a lock—otherwise they wouldn't have needed a crowbar."

"So you're saying . . . ?"

"Seems like an amateur thief—or anyway, someone who isn't that experienced."

The new lock was digital. "Joe, where's that gizmo Dad gave you?"

He handed me the microwave flashlight, and I turned it on the lock, frying its settings. The door popped open, and we were inside.

"That's vandalism, you know," Joe told me.

"I'll be sure to pay them back," I said.

I meant it too. I mean, I still had money from ATAC. And I hated to ruin the new lock—but this was important.

The school was empty and silent. Creepy, in fact. It was a weird feeling, being here when there were no kids, no teachers, and absolutely no noise.

Everything looked strangely normal, though. Lockers lined the halls, the floors looked mopped and swept—no sign of broken glass like in the elementary schools, where, according to Iola, lots of windows had been broken.

Nothing looked out of place here.

Except the whole huge room looked like a bomb had hit it!

There were tables overturned, chairs smashed and scattered everywhere—and a wide variety of rotting foods all over the floor.

And the smell was not to be believed.

"Yuck!" Joe said, covering his nose and mouth. "I can't breathe!"

Neither could I. But we had to check the crime scene out. Obviously, the police must have been over it with a fine-tooth comb. Still, in a mess like this, it would be easy to miss a clue. Even an important one.

We used our flashlights—the regular ones we always carry—and scoped out the place. Joe put a napkin over his face, but I doubt if it helped much.

As for me, I was feeling a strong urge to puke. If I had, it would have blended right in with the mess, I promise you.

"Chet said a lot of food was stolen," Joe said, between gasps for air. "They sure left a lot behind."

"You'd think someone would be in here to clean it all up."

"Yeah—some industrial-strength cleaning service."

"They must have stripped the shelves clean," I said. "Because they're empty now."

"Didn't Chet say something about them delivering a big load of food and supplies for the start of school?"

"That's right. But unless they had a big truck of their own, whoever broke in here couldn't have taken it all with them."

"Maybe they just threw it all on the floor," Joe said, "and didn't take *anything* with them."

"They probably hit the freezer, too."

"Let's check and see."

The door to the walk-in freezer was locked, but unlike the outside door to the cafeteria, this lock wasn't anything special. I had the door open in less than thirty seconds.

We pointed our flashlights inside. There were metal shelves lining each side of the long, dark room. The shelves were mostly empty, but there were quite a few boxes of frozen food scattered on the floor—most of them broken open and ruined.

"Hey, Frank. You know, the rain washed away all the footprints from outside—but there might be some in here, preserved in the frost!"

A long shot, true, but still, it was a shot.

We moved on into the pitch-dark freezer room, playing our flashlights on the floor.

We were almost to the back wall when I heard the creaking of the heavy metal door behind us.

It slammed shut with a sickening thud. Then I heard the lock click into place.

And something else—*laughter.*

JOE

13.

COLD, COLD HEART

If you've never been locked inside a walk-in freezer before, let me save you some time and a lot of discomfort—*don't try it.*

These walk-in babies are deep-freezes, with the emphasis on *deep.* Food stored in them can last for a year or more. As for human life, well, Frank and I would be lucky if we lasted an hour.

It was COLD in there! COLDCOLDCOLD-COLD!!!!!

In less than a minute, I was shivering so hard, with my whole body, that you would have thought I was having a seizure.

I'm sure Frank was feeling the same way. He was busy playing his flashlight all over the walls, looking for an escape switch that would trigger the freezer door to open.

You'd think a school system, of all places, would build in a safety escape switch. But if there was one, we sure couldn't find it.

"Um, Joe? I think we might be in trouble here," Frank finally said.

I tried ramming the door, but it didn't give, and I knew it wasn't going to, no matter how many times I tried.

Ow. The pain. The cold. Brrrrrr . . .

And on top of everything, the total *humiliation* of it! After all the times we'd cheated death, to go down in such a lame way . . .

Just think—when school finally started, the cafeteria workers would open the freezer door and find us with icicles hanging from our noses, frozen solid like a pair of gigantic popsicles! Not to mention dead. Talk about embarrassing!

"Heeellllp!!!" I screamed. "HEEELLLLP!!!"

Frank joined in, and we made one heck of a chorus—but who exactly did we think was going to help us? The fiend who'd locked us in?

I could hear him now, on the other side of the heavy steel door, laughing his head off.

The laughter was high-pitched, I noticed. So

high-pitched you'd have thought it was a woman out there. . . .

"Ha-ha! I've got you now!"

It *was* a woman!

"Let us out of here!" Frank yelled. "You don't want to be facing murder charges, do you?"

More laughter. Then, "Yeah, right. I'm not worried about it."

There was something familiar about that voice. Where had I heard it before?

"You're not getting out until the cops get here," said the voice. "I'm gonna go call them right now, and you're gonna get what's coming to you."

The cops?

"Hey . . . who *is* that?" Frank asked me.

"So what did you think, you could get away with breaking in here twice in one week?"

So *she* thought *we* were the bad guys!

Finally, I recognized the voice. "Loretta? Is that you?"

Silence from our school custodian. Then, "Who *is* that in there?"

"It's us, Loretta—Frank and Joe Hardy!"

"Huh? What are you two doing here?"

The door was thrown open, and Frank and I tumbled out into the hallway, twitching from the cold. We hopped up and down and rubbed ourselves to get warm, while Loretta stared at us like we were a pair of Martians.

"I thought you were . . . you know . . ."

"Yeah, it's okay, Loretta," Frank assured her.

"An honest mistake," I agreed.

"You boys were playing detective again, weren't you?"

Loretta Rivera has been a friend of ours for a few years now. Once or twice she's covered for us when we had to leave school in a hurry, hot on the trail of some criminal. But she's always thought of us as amateurs—and this latest escapade wasn't going to do our reputation any good.

"You boys ought to let the cops do their thing," she said, wagging a finger at us.

"Come on, Loretta," I said. "If the person behind this is a student here, we're the perfect ones to break the case."

She sighed. "Kids—you can't talk sense to them. They think they already know everything." She shook her head. "You could have died in there. I was gonna call the cops, but what if I wasn't such a nice person? What if I'd just left you to freeze?"

"We thought the school was deserted," Frank explained. "We didn't expect anyone to be around."

"Oh, well, you know me," she said with a little

smile. "I was just tidying up—you know, with all the mess here, I couldn't just leave it to rot and stink. I came in here, and it was dark, and then I saw something moving, and two shadows going into the freezer. . . . I just put two and two together, you know?"

"That's okay, Loretta," Frank said. "You did the right thing."

"No harm done," I said. "Don't feel bad. You were just trying to do the same thing we were— catch a criminal."

"I'm glad you understand," she said, relieved. "So we're still friends?"

"Totally," I said.

"Hey," Frank added, "if you see anything suspicious, could you call us?"

"Okay—*after* I call the cops."

We had just said good-bye to Loretta and stepped outside into the warm evening air when Frank's cell phone started playing its tune. He fished it out and flipped it open.

"Hello? Oh, hi, Dad. What's up?"

There was a long silence as Frank listened. "Oh . . . uh-huh . . . I see . . ."

At first he seemed relaxed, but then I saw his whole body stiffen, and I knew that this was something important.

"Okay, we'll be right there." Frank snapped the phone shut.

"Well?"

"You want the good news or the bad news?"

"Start with the good."

"Okay. Dad checked out Captain Creamy, and he really is with ATAC."

"Uh-huh. And . . . what's the bad news?"

"Remember George Guthrie?"

I nodded. Who could forget our homeless friend?

"Apparently, he walked out of the shelter last night, took all his stuff with him, didn't tell anyone where he was going, and hasn't been heard from since."

"Okay . . . but lots of homeless people do things like that. It doesn't mean—"

Frank cut me off with a wave of his hand.

"And now there's a school bus on fire at the yard!"

FRANK

14.

FAMOUS LAST WORDS

When we got to the Board of Education complex, the fire department was already there in force. Everyone seemed to be shouting at once as they hosed down the buses next to the one that was in flames.

Other firefighters were trying to get to these buses and drive them away before they exploded from the heat. It wasn't going to be easy—and it was definitely dangerous work.

Black smoke poured from the inside of the stricken bus, billowing through its shattered windows and from its engine. There wasn't much left of the bus—just a charred frame.

Dozens of bystanders were gathered around the outside of the chain-link fence, looking into the bus yard.

At the gate, Chief Collig stood with Officer Reilly and a few others. He was talking to the fire chief, who seemed distracted. Every now and then he barked orders into his walkie-talkie.

Then I saw Dad. He was out at the curb, obviously looking for someone—probably us. "Come on, Joe," I said, and we went over to him.

"Well," he said when he saw us, "so much for your instincts about George Guthrie." He looked as unhappy as I felt.

"Sorry, Dad," I said. "I guess you were right about him. We should have listened to you."

I still had trouble picturing George Guthrie as a dangerously psycho criminal. But Dad was obviously convinced, and at this point, who was I to argue with him?

"Well, the police have an all-points bulletin out on him," Dad said. "I imagine they'll catch him before too long, and that will be the end of this rash of incidents. Too bad we didn't arrest him when we had the chance."

I felt lousy. Because of me and Joe, another school bus had been destroyed, and brave men and women were now risking their lives to move other buses out of harm's way.

"Well, come on," Dad said, motioning to us. "Let's go try and find out how this happened."

We went in through the gates and tried to get as close as we could to the fire without getting in the way. It wasn't easy.

We had been there for a minute or so, just watching them douse the flames, when one of the firefighters nearest to the bus shouted, "Hey! There's someone inside!"

An instant megajolt of adrenaline went through me—but I didn't move. Not right away.

Whoever was inside the bus, I knew there was no safe way of getting him or her out. Not yet—not while flames were still blocking the doorway. I may be brave, but I'm not stupid.

Joe, on the other hand . . .

Well, let's just say it wasn't two seconds before he was climbing the rear bumper of the bus and diving in through the broken back window.

What did *I* do, you ask?

What else *could* I do? I followed Joe through the window, ignoring the shouts of alarm from the firefighters and police (Dad, too, I'm sure, although I couldn't pick out his voice).

Instantly, thick black smoke blotted out my vision, and I started coughing my guts up.

The fire was mostly out, but that didn't make it any safer. Inhaling smoke can kill you just as easily.

Assuming someone was really in here, we were

going to have to get him or her out in a hurry.

I could hear Joe coughing and gagging nearby, but I couldn't see him at all. My eyes burned something fierce every time I opened them. I kept feeling around with my hands instead, hoping to run across something human.

"Frank!" I heard Joe shout between coughs. "I've got him! Help me . . . get . . ."

The rest was lost in a cascade of coughing. But following the sound, I soon found Joe, and together we dragged the dead weight of the victim to the rear of the bus, hoisted him out the window, then tumbled out ourselves.

I fell straight to the ground, about to pass out. If a firefighter hadn't shown up with an oxygen mask just then, I might not have made it.

After a minute or so, I felt much better. That's when I saw Joe. Dad was bent over him, looking upset—but I could see that Joe was basically going to be okay.

Then I looked around to see what had happened to the guy we dragged out of the bus.

There was a knot of paramedics kneeling down in a circle. I walked over there, still woozy, and saw them giving CPR to the unconscious man.

I froze in my tracks.

It was George Guthrie!

Even a crazy man wouldn't set himself on fire, would he?

And how did he get in? I guess where there's a will, there's a way. . . .

I wished I could talk with him, ask him face-to-face. But it was too late now.

Or was it?

"Hey, he's coming around!" one of the paramedics yelled.

Sure enough, good old George started coughing and wheezing, coming back to life.

I edged closer, listening to the paramedics talking.

"Is he going to make it?" I asked one of them, a young guy with a mustache.

He looked at me and sighed. "Not likely," he said. "Burns over most of his body. Plus the lung damage. He's barely hanging on."

"I have to talk to him!"

"No way, man."

"Listen, it's really, really, REALLY important!"

"Sorry. He's on his way to the emergency room as soon as we can get the ambulance over here."

Sure enough, here came the ambulance, sirens and flashers going full blast.

With it came Joe, now walking and breathing on his own.

"What the—? Hey, it's George!"

"No kidding," I said.

Then I turned and saw that the paramedic had gone off to speak to the ambulance crew.

There wasn't a second to lose. I eased my way through the people surrounding George and knelt down beside him. Joe was right behind me.

"Hi, George," I said. "Hang in there, big guy, you're gonna make it."

It was hard to lie to him like that, but I didn't know what else to say.

He looked right through me for a second. Then he seemed to focus on my face, because his eyes opened wider. I wasn't sure, but I thought he recognized me.

His lips started moving, but I couldn't hear anything.

"What's that you're saying, George?" Joe asked.

Again, the moving lips, but no sound. I bent over closer to listen.

"Sleeping . . . in bus . . ." he whispered in my ear, in between gasps and wheezes.

I remembered George had said he had asthma. All that smoke could only have made things worse.

"George, you didn't do this, did you?" Joe asked. He shook his head weakly. "Never . . . hurt anyone . . . just . . . couldn't stand . . . living in the shelter anymore. . . ."

He winced and stopped talking.

I reached for an oxygen mask and placed it on his face so he could breathe. I didn't hold it there long, though. There was no time to lose. The paramedics were setting up the stretcher and the IV tubes. In about thirty seconds, they were going to take George Guthrie away. In his condition, I knew this might be our last chance to talk to him.

"Do you know who did it?" I asked him, getting right to the point.

His eyes drifted away, and I was afraid we were going to lose him before he could say another word. But then he seemed to recover and refocus.

"I . . . missed living on the bus . . . so I went back. . . ." he said. "I was just minding . . . my own business. . . ."

More wheezing and coughing. Our time with him was running out fast. "George—who did this to you?" I asked again.

"Somebody . . . threw something . . . through the window . . . explosion . . . fire . . ."

"Did you see who it was, George?"

He shook his head, and my heart sank. But then he said, "Heard it, though. . . ."

I came instantly to attention. "Heard what?"

"Just before the explosion . . . strange sound . . ."

"Yes?"

"Song . . ."

"Song? What song?"

He took a deep, painful breath—and then he started to sing.

"I've . . . been working on . . . the railroad. . . ."

Then a deep, rattling sound came from George Guthrie's throat—and he was gone.

15.

WE ALL SCREAM FOR ICE CREAM

I have seen people die before. It's never easy, and most times, it isn't pretty.

But watching George Guthrie die made me angrier than I'd ever felt in my entire life. Some idiot decides to set a fire somewhere, and some other poor slob gets burned to a crisp!

Ernie Bickerstaff—alias Captain Creamy—and I were definitely having words.

I heard a sniffing sound coming from nearby. I turned and saw that Frank was crying. He wiped his eyes a couple of times, but he never stopped staring at poor, dead George.

I don't cry much myself, but I knew Frank felt the same way I did.

I paid my respects to the dead—quickly—then

pulled Frank away from there before he lost it alto-gether.

Dad saw us go, but before he could come after us, Chief Collig put a hand on his shoulder and started talking to him. I could see Dad wanted to break away and come after us, but he didn't. Obvi-ously, whatever the chief was saying, it was pretty important.

After all, a man was dead. What had started out looking like a case of simple mischief was now a case of murder.

"I knew he was innocent," Frank said. His jaw was tight, and his voice was husky. "I knew it all along."

"You did, Frank. You had him pegged."

"Yeah. But I never connected all this with Cap-tain Creamy," he said, slapping himself on the forehead. "How stupid am I?"

"Hey, man, the guy's with ATAC. You had to give him the benefit of the doubt."

"No, I didn't—that's just the point! I assumed he was okay, and he wasn't."

"So did Q.T., and Dad, and everyone else at ATAC. They hired him, right? I mean, if they were fooled, how can you blame yourself?"

"Joe, they hired you and me because we under-stand teens better than they do—or we're *supposed* to, anyway."

He stared right through me. "We should have known, Joe. We should have. No getting around it. We just plain blew it."

What could I say? He was right.

"Well, at least we can help bring Ernie Bickerstaff to justice," I said.

"All the clues were there, right in front of us," Frank said. "Remember he said he was having money problems?"

"Yeah? So?"

"He must have vandalized the schools and the buses to delay the opening of school, so that he could keep selling ice cream right into September."

"For that, he goes and kills somebody?" I was about ready to explode with rage.

"No. Remember, Ernie didn't know George was inside that bus. He was just up to more of the same mischief—except this time, he messed up royally."

"Hey, remember how he robbed the cafeteria freezer?" I said. "It would have been full of ice cream, right?"

"Right! Good thinking, Joe. I don't remember seeing any ice cream in there, do you?"

"Now that you mention it, no."

"And remember he said he was a computer programmer—that he did that kind of thing for ATAC?"

"Yeah?"

"He must have created the fake missions for us himself, just to get us out of town while he committed his crimes. A guy like him would know exactly how to do it."

I looked at Frank, and he looked back at me.

"Well, what are we waiting for?" I said. "Let's go get him!"

"Don't you think we should tell the police what George told us?"

"Fine." That's Frank for you.

So we went over to Dad and Chief Collig and told them what George had told us.

"That's a very fine theory," the chief said. "There's just one problem."

"Problem?" I repeated.

"Yes. You've got no proof. None at all."

Frank's jaw dropped. I'm sure mine was down to the floor as well.

"But—George said he heard the song. . . ."

"Your friend George was a little bit loony, if you didn't notice," Chief Collig pointed out. "From what they told us at the shelter, he had quite a history of mental illness."

I wanted to say something to protest, but I could see it wouldn't do any good. Chief Collig and the Department were determined to put an end to this rash of incidents. And there was no quicker way to do it than to blame George Guthrie—a dead man—for everything.

Well, that would be just fine and dandy, at least until the next time school property got trashed. The trouble was, Frank and I believed George Guthrie. And if we were right, it meant George's killer was still out there.

Not okay.

"What are we going to do now, Frank?" I asked as we walked away from the crime scene.

"There's only one thing to do, Joe. We've got to track down Captain Creamy ourselves and make him confess to his crimes."

Ha! Easier said than done. We had no address or phone number for a Captain Creamy, or even for Ernie Bickerstaff. A quick call to Information revealed that the number—and address—were unlisted.

"We ought to go home and get our bikes," I suggested. "We could cover a big slice of Bayport in a couple of hours that way—and if one of us finds the truck, he can call the other on his cell phone."

"Good idea, Joe—but we'll be able to cover even more ground if we have help."

He punched in Chet Morton's number. "Hi, Chet, Frank here. Listen, we need you to help us out, okay? Yeah, right now . . . you're eating dinner? What time is it?"

I checked my watch. It was dinnertime, all right. Six o'clock on the nose. We only had a couple of hours till sunset, and a whole lot of ground to cover!

Frank was busy explaining to Chet how we wanted him to search the streets in his car. He got his license a couple of months ago and has access to a nice set of wheels.

"You'd better get Iola and Callie in on this too," Frank said. "Yeah, I know they don't drive yet—but they can each go jogging on a different route. . . . We need as many people on the lookout as we can get. I know it's last minute, but this is important, okay?"

Frank finally got Chet to skip the rest of his meal and get moving—not an easy task.

"Okay, let's go, Joe. You cover the east side of downtown, I'll get the west side. We can meet up at the corner of Main and Maple."

Enough said. I took off on my bike, looking for the innocent-looking ice-cream truck that harbored a maniacal murderer.

Now, Bayport is a big town—or a small city, depending on how you look at it. Either way, there's a lot of ground to cover. It took me almost an hour to scour the streets of my half of downtown. I didn't find anything—until I hit Maple Street.

And there it was—the Captain Creamy truck! Straight ahead of me, playing its jolly tune. I roared up behind it, waited till it stopped at a traffic light, then got off my bike and ran up to the driver's door. I yanked it open and dragged the driver out into the street.

"HEY!! What are you doing?"

Oops. This driver was a girl. Wrong truck.

"Sorry," I said, and let her go.

Back on my bike, and feeling mighty stupid, I headed for my meet-up with Frank.

"Any luck?" I asked him.

"No. How 'bout you?"

"Nope." I decided not to tell him about my little mistake. Too embarrassing. But it did teach me something—there was more than one Captain Creamy truck. I mean, I guess I knew that, but now I'd been reminded—in the worst possible way.

We mapped out another search grid, but an hour later, when we'd finished, there was still no sign of our quarry.

A quick phone call to Chet told us that he hadn't had any luck either. Neither had Callie or Iola.

And now it was getting dark.

"This isn't cool," I said.

"No, you're right," Frank agreed. "And now, all the trucks are probably going back to the warehouse for the night."

Wait a minute. . . .

"The warehouse!" we both said at once.

We didn't know where it was, but a quick visit to a pay phone in a nearby restaurant told us that the Captain Creamy Ice Cream Company was located at 1511 Parker Boulevard.

"If we get over there right away, we might catch him returning his truck for the night," I said.

"Great. Ever heard of Parker Boulevard?"

I hadn't, but the mechanic over at the Pump'N'Go gas station knew where it was. He gave us directions, and we roared out of there, leaving a cloud of dust behind us.

There wasn't a moment to lose. If we missed Captain Creamy, he would have another whole night to wreak havoc on Bayport. More lives might be lost, more damage done.

We couldn't let that happen!

Parker Boulevard was in an industrial zone at the far south end of town. No wonder we'd never heard of it. The buildings here were huge, with no windows. It wasn't a place where people lived, and at night, the whole neighborhood was plain spooky.

We spotted the Captain Creamy building easily enough. There were four ice-cream trucks parked right out front, and a gigantic ice-cream cone was mounted on the roof.

"This must be the place," Frank said as we pulled over and parked our bikes.

"Let's go do this thing," I said, cracking my knuckles.

I was ready for action, primed for a fight. I wanted to punch Ernie Bickerstaff's lights out—for poor old George's sake.

The only trouble was, there was nobody around. It seemed like we'd arrived too late. All the trucks had been returned for the night, and no one answered when we rang the buzzer at the gate.

"Now what?" I asked.

Frank thought for a minute. "We could wait till morning, and show up here before he comes to get his truck."

"*If* he comes."

"What do you mean?"

"Well, if he reads the morning paper and finds out that the fire he set killed somebody, he might get spooked and not show up."

"Good thinking, Joe. Well, I guess we'd better go

in and have a look around—maybe we can find some evidence."

I pulled out the microwave flashlight we'd borrowed from Dad, and shone it on the security camera that was focused on the gate. It took about six seconds before the camera started smoking and sparking.

So much for security. I handed Frank the flashlight and hopped the fence. Frank followed, and we headed for the parked trucks.

There were six of them in all, once we found the two on the far side of the building. Peering through the windows, we soon found the truck we were looking for—computer gear was scattered all over the passenger seat. It had to be the right one!

Frank took out his lock pick and jimmied the door, while I kept an eye out for security guards, or anybody else who might be around.

What we were doing here was technically illegal, and while we might not wind up in jail for it, the folks at ATAC would not be happy if they had to come bail us out and explain what we were doing there.

We got inside the truck, and Frank started sifting through the computer CDs and drives. I'm not sure what he was looking for, and I don't think he knew either. He pocketed a few likely-looking disks and then said, "Let's go inside."

"Inside?"

"Into the warehouse."

"You think we're going to find evidence in there?"

He shrugged. "We're already here, Joe. And you never know where a clue might be hidden."

True.

We left the truck and headed for the warehouse door.

Again the lock pick. Again the microwave flashlight to fry the security system.

"I sure hope ATAC will pay for the damage we're causing," I said.

"We'll worry about that later, okay?" he said as he shoved the door open and we entered the pitch-dark warehouse.

16.

THE BIG CHILL

It was dark inside the warehouse—dark and silent—
but the first thing that hit us was the cold.

We'd been running around looking for Ernie,
working up a sweat on a hot summer night, and
now here we were, in our T-shirts, entering the
world of frozen treats. I started shivering after
about thirty seconds, and I'm sure Joe did too.

We'd been locked in Bayport High's freezer just
a few hours ago, and I thought when Loretta let us
out that that would be the last time in my life I'd be
so cold.

Wrong.

I felt in the pockets of my cargo pants, just to
make sure I had my cell phone, to call the cops
once we nailed Captain Creamy.

Check.

Swiss Army knife?

Got it.

Okay, I was ready for whatever came next.

Joe was busy playing his flashlight around the dim warehouse. Huge vats, ten feet across, were sunk halfway into the floor. Most were covered with steel lids, but one was open to view.

Joe shone his beam down into it. The vat was empty. On the bottom was a giant propeller for stirring ice cream as it slowly froze. The propeller was attached to a steel pole in the center of the vat.

"Whoa," I said, staring down into it. "I'd hate to get stuck in one of these when it's making ice cream."

Joe shuddered. Maybe it was what I said, or maybe it was just the cold.

We moved on into the warehouse, past tubs of ingredients and freezers full of finished product in all different flavors.

One of the tubs had a skull and crossbones on it. "Geez," Joe said. "What kind of poison do they put in ice cream?" He shone his beam lower on the tub. "Vanillin? What's that?"

"Artificial vanilla," I told him.

"It's poison?"

"If you eat enough of it. I wouldn't worry about

a cone's worth, but you might want to try the naturally flavored vanilla. I always do."

He stared at me, annoyed. "How come you know so much about everything?"

I smiled back at him. "It's called paying attention in chemistry class. You should try it some time."

Zing!

"Besides," I added, "vanilla's my favorite flavor, remember?"

"Okay, genius. If you're so smart, what do we do now?"

"We search this place high and low."

"For what? He's obviously not here. Are we supposed to hang out in this icebox till morning?"

He was right. Another hour in here and frostbite would start to set in.

"We could check the office files. They might have a folder on him with his address and phone number."

"Or we could just call Dad and get him to look it up for us," Joe pointed out.

I smiled and pulled out my cell phone. "Now who's the genius?"

Except that there was no reception. The warehouse was in a dead zone.

"Great. Just great," I said, putting the phone back in my pocket. "Remind me to complain to customer service."

"So where's the office?" Joe asked, getting us back on track. He shone his light all around, and there it was, right next to the door where we'd come in.

We headed back that way, past the rows of vats. Now I noticed that hanging over them, suspended from a grid, were several huge hoses made of flexible plastic. HOT FUDGE, was written on one, BUTTERSCOTCH on another.

"This place is so cool!" Joe said.

"Yeah, in more ways than one," I said, shivering some more.

We passed another open vat. Then I stopped in my tracks.

Something was wrong.

"Whazzup, dude?" Joe asked.

I walked back to the open vat. "Rocky Road," I said, reading the sign on the side of it. "Yuck."

"Are you kidding? Rocky Road rules!"

"I know, I know, it's your all-time favorite," I said. "But *look*, Joe."

"Huh?"

"Point your flashlight into the vat."

He did. "It's got ice cream in it. So?"

"Why would they leave the vat open if it wasn't empty? I mean, the ice cream's liable to spoil."

"Probably somebody just forgot."

"Maybe."

Or maybe not.

The sudden sound of running footsteps behind us made Joe and me spin around—and just as we did, someone barreled straight into us!

"OOF!"

We both fell backward into the vat!

SPLAT!

Suddenly, we were drowning in a sea of soft ice cream—Rocky Road, no less!

17.

DEAD ZONE

I fell flat on my back into a vat of Rocky Road. Next thing I knew, I couldn't breathe.

Don't ever try swimming in a vat of ice cream— even soft ice cream. For one thing, it's freezing cold. For another, it's as thick as mud, and really hard to move around in.

Lucky for me and Frank, it was only waist deep. Soon we were able to stand up and wipe the stuff out of our eyes.

We found ourselves staring up into the laughing face of Ernie Bickerstaff—alias Captain Creamy!

"HAHAHAHAHA!!" he cackled, clapping his hands. "Two with one shot! Ex-cellent!" He rubbed his hands together in maniacal glee and laughed some more.

This guy made Peter Nutt and poor George Guthrie look normal. I mean, he was really out of his mind.

I tried moving toward him, but it wasn't much use. The ice cream had the consistency of quicksand.

"So sorry," Ernie said, putting his palms together. "I didn't plan to kill anyone—least of all a couple of fellow ATAC agents."

"How can you do this?" Frank asked. "You're supposed to be fighting crime, not *committing* it!"

Ernie made a sad clown face. "So sorry," he repeated. "But you know, if people are so stupid, they deserve what they get."

"Ernie," I said, "let us out of here, and we'll see that you get a fair trial."

"Oh, right . . . let me see . . . that would let me out of prison, with good behavior, in, say . . . ten years?"

I didn't answer him. But he was right.

"The police are on their way here!" Frank said suddenly.

"Oh, no, they're not," Ernie shot back. "I was monitoring police radio in the truck on the way here. And this place has no cell phone reception, so . . ."

Frank's face was getting redder by the minute.

"You'll never get away with this!" he shouted.

"Maybe not, but at least I'll have a fighting chance. If I let you go, it's curtains for me."

Now it was Frank's turn to be speechless.

"It's nothing personal," Ernie explained. "I actually like you two guys. Unlike most kids at the high school, you never made fun of me when I was in the chicken suit. I remember little kindnesses like that."

"Aw, you're breakin' my heart," I said, annoyed. "So now you're going to kill us?"

"You're on to me," he replied. "What choice do I have—keeping in mind that prison is not an option?"

He walked over to a cement pillar. I saw what he was going for: the switchbox.

I thought of the sharp propeller blades somewhere on the bottom of the vat—blades that would slice us to pieces once they got going.

Ernie seemed to read my mind. "Don't worry," he said. "I'm not going to slice and dice you. You'll die a painless death—slowly freezing until you're numb. . . ."

He flicked a switch, and the hoses overhead started moving. A large one stopped right over our heads. Ernie flicked another switch, and more

Rocky Road started pouring down into the vat.

"There you go," said Ernie. "Like I said. Painless. Your body temperatures will just drop until your vital organs stop working and freeze solid."

He stood at the edge of the vat. "I really am sorry," he said. "Sorry for betraying ATAC. Sorry about all the damage I did. Sorry the homeless guy died. Sorriest of all about killing you guys."

For a minute there, I thought he was actually going to burst into tears.

He might as well have.

"I wish I'd been able to go to college. . . . I wish I could earn a good living legally. . . ."

Then suddenly, his face seemed to harden into an angry mask. "I wish a lot of things—but it's all ATAC's fault! If I hadn't skipped college to be a crime fighter, I'd have been okay."

He got to his feet and stared down at us, taking one last look. "You see, crime *does* pay," he said. "It's crime fighting that doesn't!"

And then he burst out laughing again. "HAHA-HAHAHA!!!!"

He bent over double, turning away from us. Taking advantage of the moment, I looked at Frank. I saw that he was motioning to me, pretending to fire a gun.

Oh! Right! The stun gun—I'd been carrying it in the pockets of my cargo pants all this time!

I reached down and pulled out the pieces, wiping them off on my arms and fitting them together as I went. Just as I was ready to fire, Captain Creamy saw what I was up to.

I thought he'd duck, but he just stood there.

I pulled the trigger—

Nothing.

I pulled again. Same story.

Ernie burst out laughing again.

"This thing's useless!" I moaned to Frank.

"Of course it's useless!" Ernie said. "I'm the one who gave it to you, remember? HAHAHAHA!!!"

Okay, that was it. We were going to die. I was sure of it—so sure that I didn't care anymore what happened.

"ARRGGHH!"

I took my useless weapon and flung it at Ernie Bickerstaff as hard as I could. It hit him smack in the forehead, and he went down like a pile of bricks!

"Now *that* is nonlethal force!" I said.

"Ah, yes," Frank agreed, "the ATAC code: Never kill if you don't have to."

"Stupid weapon," I said.

"Well, at least it was good for something."

Then it hit me.

"I am such an idiot!" I smacked myself on the forehead.

"Why's that?"

"Our only hope for getting out of here was talking Captain Creamy into changing his mind. Now we're doomed for sure!"

"Oh, I don't know about that."

"Huh?"

Frank gave me a smile and a wink. Then he reached into his pocket and pulled out our dad's tiny microwave flashlight.

He wiped it off on his sleeve, aimed it at the switchbox, and five seconds later, it exploded.

Instantly, the hose stopped pouring. The sound of the motor went dead.

"Great," I said. "Now what?"

"Huh?"

"We're still gonna freeze in here."

"Not if the battery on this thing holds up." Frank turned the microwave beam on the ice cream in the vat, and instantly, it started to bubble.

You wouldn't believe how fast ice cream melts in a microwave! In less than ten minutes we were able to move again. Another five minutes, and we'd made it to the edge of the vat and hauled ourselves out.

We stared down at Captain Creamy, who was just starting to stir.

"Got any cuffs on you?" Frank asked me.

"I've got a belt," I said.

"That'll do."

18.

BACK TO SCHOOL

For once our whole family was seated around the dinner table. It was a Sunday night in the middle of September. Tomorrow, two weeks late, would be the first day of school.

Not something we usually celebrate, but this year was different. Everyone in Bayport—even Brian Conrad—was happy things were finally getting back to normal.

Thanks to lots of publicity, the whole town had shown up at George Guthrie's funeral. Donations to the homeless had gone through the roof. And Ernie Bickerstaff was safely behind bars.

"I don't think they should make anyone dress up in chicken suits anymore," Aunt Trudy said. "It's insulting to chickens."

"Aaarrkk! Pretty bird! Pretty bird!" Playback squawked, and hopped from Aunt Trudy's shoulder to the top of her head.

She ignored him—her very own spoiled brat—and kept on talking. "It's bad for people's self-esteem as well. No wonder he turned into a murderer."

In the news there had been no mention of Joe's and my involvement in the case. As usual, ATAC rhymes with anonymous. All Aunt Trudy knew was what everyone in town knew—that a young man had gone crazy and done crazy things.

It was over now, but people were still buzzing about it—and would be for a long time to come.

"Time for dessert," Mom said, getting up and going into the kitchen.

"Mmmm, I can't wait!" I said. Whenever we have a celebration, Trudy makes the salad, Dad cooks dinner, and Mom does dessert—and it's always something spectacular.

Mom came back in carrying a beautiful cake, iced in chocolate, with two lit candles in it. HAPPY END OF SUMMER was written in white icing.

"Yum!" I said. "Looks fantastic, Mom!"

"What kind of cake is it?" Joe asked eagerly.

"Ice-cream cake!" Mom said.

Doh!

"Um, no thanks, Mom," I said.

"I'm stuffed," Joe agreed.

"But Joe, it's Rocky Road—your favorite!" Mom said.

"I . . . I'm just not hungry for ice cream right now," Joe said. "Sorry."

Poor Mom. She looked so disappointed!

But there was no way on earth Joe was ever eating Rocky Road again.

And that went double for me.

"AARRK!" Playback squawked. "We all scream for ice cream!"

DON'T MISS THE HARDY BOYS ADVENTURES IN COMICS!

ALL NEW STORIES!
ALL NEW FULL COLOR COMICS
a new one every 3 months

Already out:
Graphic Novel #1
"The Ocean of Osyria"
ISBN 1-59707-001-7
Graphic Novel #2
"Identity Theft"
Beginning an all-new direction for the Hardy Boys, reflecting the storylines in the upcoming Simon & Schuster revamped Hardy Boys novels, who or what is the mysterious organization known as A.T.A.C.? And how are Frank, Joe, and even Fenton Hardy involved? Are the Hardys leaving Bayport forever? How has Laura Hardy's life changed? Why is Aunt Gertrude acting so strange? Where's Lola and Callie? Uncover the clues to these questions and more as Frank and Joe take to the skies to crack a diamond-smuggling team of skydivers and then encounter a young woman whose identity has been stolen – literally! Or at least that's what a young woman claiming to be Joy Gallagher claims – that another girl is now living her life, with her friends, her family, and in her body! Action, thrills, and lots of mystery!
ISBN 1-59707-003-3

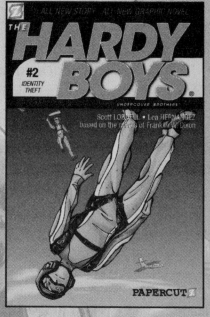

Graphic Novel #3: "Mad House"
ISBN 1-59707-010-6
All: Pocket sized, 96pp., full color, $7.95

PAPERCUTZ

At your store or order at: 555 8th Ave., Ste. 1202, New York, NY 10018, 1-800-886-1223 (M-F 9-6 EST)
MC, VISA, Amex accepted, add $3 P&H for 1st item, $1 each additional.